The

HOUND *of* FLORENCE

Also by Felix Salten

Bambi
Bambi's Children
Renni the Rescuer
A Forest World

The HOUND of FLORENCE

BAMBI'S CLASSIC ANIMAL TALES

FELIX SALTEN

Translation by HUNTLEY PATERSON

Aladdin

New York London Toronto Sydney New Delhi

This book is a work of fiction. Any references to historical events, real people, or real places are used fictitiously. Other names, characters, places, and events are products of the author's imagination, and any resemblance to actual events or places or persons, living or dead, is entirely coincidental.

ALADDIN
An imprint of Simon & Schuster Children's Publishing Division
1230 Avenue of the Americas, New York, NY 10020
This Aladdin hardcover edition June 2014

Also available in an Aladdin paperback edition.
For information about special discounts for bulk purchases,
please contact Simon & Schuster Special Sales at 1-866-506-1949
or business@simonandschuster.com.
The Simon & Schuster Speakers Bureau can bring authors to your live
event. For more information or to book an event contact
the Simon & Schuster Speakers Bureau at 1-866-248-3049
or visit our website at www.simonspeakers.com.
Jacket design by Karin Paprocki
Interior design by Hilary Zarycky
The text of this book was set in Yana.
Manufactured in the United States of America 0514 FFG
2 4 6 8 10 9 7 5 3 1
Library of Congress Control Number 2013956891
ISBN 978-1-4424-8749-9 (hc)
ISBN 978-1-4424-8748-2 (pbk)
ISBN 978-1-4424-8750-5 (eBook)

If so be thou art poor on this earth,
thou must be a dog for one half of thy life;
then mayest thou spend the other half
as a man among men.
—The Hermit of Amiata

LUCAS GRASSI STOLE OUT OF THE gloomy old house in the Tuchlauben without a word of farewell. Within the cramped walls of a building into which the sun but rarely shone, he was leaving his belongings and the last years of his boyhood. In the kitchen, the bedroom and the parlour, even in the windings of the steep familiar stairs, which he was now descending never to climb again, in the dark narrow passage along which he strode for the last time, he was leaving all he knew and loved on earth. In every nook and cranny of the place there were traces of his father which had kept the memory of the old man green and fresh; for he had never left these rooms altogether; his presence haunted them and stood beside his son with a semblance of life that was only slowly and hardly perceptibly fading away.

Whenever Lucas called to mind how his father's hands had rested on the table, or raised the window-bolt above it and then carefully stretched the parchment across the drawing-board, or how every morning he had seen him sit up in his bed in the recess, his pale calm face visible in the twilight of the room, his gentle voice uttering his first greeting and asking the first question before starting on a new day, he always felt that at any moment his father might come into the room through the low, rusty-black door.

But Lucas Grassi knew that all this was now at an end. He saw only too well that it was impossible for him to remain in the old place any longer, for he had not even the wherewithal to appease his hunger, much less to pay his arrears of rent. It seemed to him almost a stroke of luck that he had been able to find, near the Kärtner wall, a wretched attic which he had found no difficulty in renting for a mere song. But at that moment, as he stepped out into the street from the old house, he was conscious of a momentary feeling of pained astonishment to think that he was leaving his home, precisely as he had done so often—oh, how often!—before, but that now it was forever, without a word of farewell!

He was still very young, and did not know how frequently a man stands all unknowing on the threshold of a new life, his back to a past forever closed. He did not know that, at such important moments, the uninterrupted forward march of Fate leaves but little time for farewell, or that possibly it was all for the best that this should be so; nor was he aware that his momentary feeling of pained astonishment was in itself a leave-taking.

He wandered slowly and uncertainly along the Tuchlauben, caught up and borne along by the busy bustle of the day, ambling on, as every man does who has no goal, no hope, and is bowed down by care. The feeling of bitterness, which had oppressed him ever since his father's death, seemed to gnaw more sharply than ever at his heart. His ears were deaf to the sing-song of the street hawkers, or the warning shouts of the runners, who, clad in gorgeous liveries, spread commotion right and left as they dashed forward in front of the various coaches. He did not even notice the coaches as they rocked and rattled past.

On that day when Lucas Grassi set out to meet his destiny, there were doubtless many others in Vienna as poor as himself. But only a few felt their poverty as acutely as he did, as intolerable torture. At such moments, when his soul rose up in impotent revolt, he hated even the city itself, which, with its bastions and moats seemed, as it were, to hold him imprisoned in a dismal dungeon, and, flaunting its riches in his face, to torment and make mock of him. He hated the narrow pavements in the streets. Hemmed in on either side by houses gray with age, dark and tortuous, they seemed always to lead back to the same spot.

He longed to be off to the beautiful land of sunshine, which he fancied he remembered having seen in early childhood. Ever since he had been left alone in Vienna, his mind had been full of it, and the faint stirrings of a new feeling of home-sickness seemed to have invaded his heart. But what his imagination pictured was not a memory of something he had really seen so much as the visions his fancy fashioned from all his father had told him. His early childhood days had been reflected in his father's stories, as a bright landscape is mirrored in a glass globe. He saw gardens full of roses and lilies, rich green trees laden with golden fruit, and houses with hospitable wide open doors beckoning the guest, their white walls gleaming like a bright smile amid the foliage. There were many other children, too, playing about in the meadows. The air was full of the plaintive songs of birds, borne on the soft summer breeze, and the warm rays of the kindly sun spread courage and good cheer all around. He could never remember how it all came about, but suddenly all these scenes vanished, his mother's form faded away, the gardens were swallowed up, and he was wandering over hill and dale by his father's side. True, it all seemed very long ago. He remembered that on their way they had sometimes been accompanied by strangers, and women he had never seen before took care of him; but they were mere shadows in his memory, and seemed to have no faces.

Towns, cornfields, valleys and wooded heights flashed past; he had no notion what or where they were. Sometimes the road ran along the banks of strange rivers. Although that journey was now nothing but a motley chain of pictures which for the most part had grown quite pale and faint, occasionally one of them would stand out distinctly, until the chain ended in the landscape that now surrounded him and over which leaden clouds so often lowered for days at a time.

As he looked back on his short life, he could not help thinking that from the very beginning it had been nothing more than a path leading from bright sunshine to impenetrable gloom, until at last this city had reared its walls about him, to crush him beneath their weight.

As he walked along the gloomy alley of the

Kohlmarkt it occurred to him again that he might look up one of his father's old colleagues, and beg for food and work. But the thought, as ever, was distasteful to him. He knew but little of his father's fellow-craftsmen; they had come to the city to build and decorate the Palace of some great noble. One or two of them were sculptors like his father, others were painters. Lucas had already heard what most of them had to say to him. They told him that, though it was not his fault, he knew nothing, for the things to which they referred could not be learned in this country. The best thing was to return to his native land, whence all of them, including his father, had come, bringing their arts with them. Otherwise the only career open to him was that of an unskilled laborer. Work of this kind they undertook to find for him, so that for the time being at least he might be self-supporting. Lucas was in want of bread, but such work he scorned, revolting against it as an intolerable means for merely keeping body and soul together. If life depended on such wretched work it was not worth living. It was absurd for a man to humble himself to the level of the day-laborer for the sake of a crust of bread. His youth rose up in arms at the idea that there was no other way out. At all events he would remain resolute, and wait stubbornly for circumstances to force his hand. He would see how long he could hold out, before poverty and hunger succeeded in breaking him.

At the corner, where the Kohlmarkt empties into the little square in front of St. Michael's Church, Lucas was suddenly brought to a standstill. The halberds of a troop of Imperial Bodyguards barred the way. Against this living fence a fairly large crowd of common people was already inquisitively pressing. Lucas quickly elbowed his way to the front. At once he surmised that some court pageant was about to take place; he loved the picturesque charm of these gorgeous and stately processions, and all unconsciously he also loved the vague yearning that such a spectacle kindled to flame in his breast.

Suddenly there was a flourish of trumpets, the clatter and beat of horses' hooves broke on the ear, and from the maze of houses concealing the gates of the

Imperial Palace, a troop of cuirassiers poured forth in a shimmering array of color, advancing to the strains of a military band. Close upon their heels came two heavy state coaches, rocking on their high-strung springs, the horses prancing beneath their trappings, impatient to break into a trot. On their boxes the coachmen calmly held the reins, while from the small windows of the coaches proud, composed faces looked down disdainfully on the mob. After them there was a gap in the procession, and Lucas, who noticed that the Bodyguards in front of him were standing more stiffly than ever to attention, concluded that the principal figure of the pageant was about to appear. Then a double row of lithe, brightly clad runners dashed lightly forward, their waving, snow-white ostrich plumes giving them the appearance of actors performing a feat. The Bodyguards presented arms with their halberds and stood massed like pillars of stone as a glittering golden coach, drawn by six huge white horses, rattled into view. Their bits sparkled with foam; nobly they tossed their heads; their powerful white bodies gleamed in the sun.

Lucas gazed upon the scene with irresistible delight, listening to the comments of the crowd.

"It's the Archduke Ludwig who's being sent to Florence."

"Yes, they say he has a weak chest and has to go to a sunny climate."

"He's not going all that way for a bit of sunshine," observed another with a laugh, "there's a marriage in the offing. . . ."

"Nonsense! He's going on a secret mission. . . ."

Still others whispered eagerly, "But we know all about Archduke Ludwig. . . . We don't need to be told what he's up to. . . . They're banishing him from Court!"– "To Florence?"–"I don't know about that . . . possibly to Florence!"

Florence!

The word sank into his heart, stirring him as it always did. He whispered it softly to himself. It hovered above him like a star of good fortune, it called to him with a cadence full of wondrous expectation and painful, urgent longing. He cast a rapid glance at the royal coach, hardly noticing the coachman or the four lackeys standing behind in their magnificent Spanish livery, like marble statues of slaves, fittings in human form, which stirred only when they were wanted.

Inside, deep in satin cushions, a slim young man in black velvet sat erect. His face was pale and drawn. Framed in ebony locks about his neck was the delicate down of some dusky fur. He held his head high and maintained a reserved and distant air, looking like some jewel locked up behind the clear crystal panes of his coach, to be gazed upon but not approached or touched.

"Why doesn't he drive straight out through the gates by the Burgbastei?" enquired one.

"He wants to say a *paternoster* at the Church of the Capucines before he leaves," was one solemn explanation, while a third vouchsafed the opinion that the Burgtor was out of the question, as the road to the south left the city at the Kärntnertor.

Softly, dreamily, Lucas whispered the word "Florence."

Close beside the Archduke's coach there ran a dog. Lucas suddenly caught sight of the animal and was filled with admiration. He was of a breed rarely seen in Vienna. Long-legged and very slim, with a long thin muzzle, he resembled a grayhound, though he was much bigger. His coat was long and curly and his bushy tail waved like a pennant in the breeze. His back gleamed like burnished gold, his flanks, chest and neck were silky white, while from brow to nose ran a narrow white streak between two patches of gold. Apparently he was of an exotic Russian breed, a prince of the hunting field. Lucas gazed intently at him, noting the noble grace of his slender legs as he haughtily trotted by, and observing that he kept close to the door of the coach glancing expectantly up at the crystal panes.

Slowly the coach rolled by. A troop of cuirassiers brought up the rear, followed by a string of heavily laden mule-wagons, rattling and bumping over the cobbles. Lucas did not wait to see the end of the procession. Suddenly turning away, reluctantly, he pushed through the crowd and made off in a different direction, as though he were in a hurry.

Shall I always remain a prisoner here? he asked

himself. Shall I always go on living alone, helpless, poor,
friendless, year in, year out until I die? Round the corner a crowd of wealthy idlers are making their way to
Florence, and I can only stand and look on, rooted to
the spot! They will drive there free as the wind, resting
when they are weary, sleeping under the shade of the
forest trees, or on the banks of silver streams, and one
day they will be in Florence, they will be wandering
about her streets, as if it were all a matter of course!
And what will it mean to them—to be in Florence? Oh!
I suppose they'll find it attractive and entertaining
enough, and the climate most agreeable; but otherwise
it will mean nothing! Absolutely nothing! What can
they do there, which they could not do just as well here?
Do they expect to find anything in Florence that they
could not get just as easily in Vienna? And I must stay
here—I, whose home is there, I who could find there the
teachers I cannot obtain here. There I could learn all
I want to learn—I could paint, model, draw, carve, and
find out how stones and metals are worked, how. . . .
Oh! I could learn everything, could see with my own

eyes everything that good craftsmen have created there from time immemorial!

In his excitement Lucas had been striding along at a tremendous pace, but as his wretchedness and despair gained the upper hand, his step slackened. Oh, well, he sighed, how can a poor devil like me hope to hear of anything? I never see anybody, never dare talk to any-body! If only I had known the Archduke was going to Florence, I should have offered myself as a servant, a stable-boy, anything, no matter what! If only they had taken me with them! I could even envy the dog who is allowed to go along, and get his regular food, and a bed at night, and who will see Florence. . . .

Snow was beginning to fall in small flakes. As Lucas looked up at the narrow ribbon of sky between the houses, he could feel its gentle touch on his cheeks. Suddenly he pulled himself together. As soon as the winter was over, he would find his way to Florence; he was determined on that. As soon as it was warm enough to sleep out in the open again and walk barefoot, he would go out by the city-gate and take the road leading

south. He would even beg—what of it? He would walk
on until his feet were sore, and at night bury himself in
the woods. And if he fell ill on the way, he would lie out
in the open until the warm rays of the sun had healed
him; and at last he *must* reach his goal!

In his abstraction he had all unconsciously been
walking faster and faster, and he now found himself on
the bastion before the house in which he was to live.

From the narrow arch of the porch a woman came
out to him. Lucas had seen her before, and knew that she
was the porter's wife. He felt grateful to her because she
had received him so kindly and had assured him with a
smile that he need not worry about the rent for the attic.
And as she caught sight of him now, she smiled again,
just as she had done the first time they had met. She was
still young, and her exuberant youth and health seemed
to be bursting the very seams of her dress.

"Well, here I am . . ." said Lucas.

She nodded, took rapid stock of him and pointed
discreetly to the portfolio he was carrying.

"Is that all?"

Lucas did not answer. He had put a few of his father's best drawings in the portfolio, together with one or two of his own attempts. That was really all he possessed in the world.

The woman looked kindly at him, as though she did not expect any answer and regarded his poverty as of no moment. It was a gentle, understanding and reassuring look.

"Go right in," she said, jerking her head over her shoulder toward the house. "You know where it is."

Lucas stepped past her and vanished up the passage. The woman stood looking after him as though he were caught in a trap.

Slowly he climbed the steep, winding stairs. They were so dark that at first, until his eyes grew accustomed to the dim light and he could discern the shadowy forms of the stone steps, he groped his way inch by inch. He had not seen the glance the woman sent after him as he entered the house, nor had he any idea why they had been so ready to rent him the top attic without making any stipulation about payment. True, it was squalid enough, but it had a bed, a table and a chair, so that at any rate he would have a roof over his head and a place of refuge at a moment when he had been afraid he would have to sleep in the street. The woman's friendly smile had made him feel, as on the first occasion, that these people had seen how poor he was and wanted to do him a kindness.

He had taken this almost as a matter of course and thought no more about it. He had not the faintest idea that he was being used merely to dispel, by means of his harmless presence, the attic's evil reputation. He did not know that a week previously, in this same bare room which he had just entered, a mysterious old man had died a mysterious death. For many years this old man had lived there alone, feared by his neighbours, regarded by everybody with silent dread, understood by none. He was very tall and pale, and so thin that in his long, loose robes, he looked more like a spirit than a creature of flesh and blood. So colorless was his face that it might have belonged to a corpse, and his every movement and step were so feeble that it seemed as though a breath would blow him away. But through the snow-white hair of his mustache and beard there gleamed the fine cupid's bow of his red lips, eternally closed, like a symbol of imperishable youth; and the clear, commanding expression of his gray eyes was that of a man of great power and vitality.

The porter's wife could remember him from the time when she was a child and used to play with other children on the bastion. Everybody, young and old alike, shrank from him. No one had ever been known to hear him speak. Silent and solitary, he walked amid his fellows, inaccessible and heedless of all about him. Often for weeks at a time he would disappear, and then as suddenly return. Everyone thought him a magician. One or two brave spirits, imagining he was versed in the occult sciences, and perhaps possessed the power of healing or exorcising serious afflictions, had, from time to time, sought his help; but to all their questions he had answered never a word, until at last, cowed by the power of his eyes, they had fled in terror from his presence. It was a long time ago that all this had happened and no one had been able to pluck up courage to address him since. Then suddenly, about a week previously, he had been found up in the attic a disfigured corpse. Thus the room came to be regarded as a place of horror, where in all probability it was neither safe nor wise to live. It was hoped that the young lodger would be a means of testing whether the old man's spirit still haunted the place.

But of all this Lucas, as he entered the tiny room, knew nothing. Laying his portfolio on the table, he cast a rapid glance round without seeing anything and then gave himself up to his thoughts. They were the thoughts of a man for whom all the world's treasures lie out of reach, a man without a calling, sitting with empty hands and staring desperately into vacancy with the one question ringing in his heart—What shall I do? What shall I do? If a definite answer is forthcoming, all anxiety vanishes instantly, the barren hours that before had stretched like a desert to the horizon, are barren no more, but full of duties, plans, hopes and even confidence, and the fingers, itching to set to work on the task that lies ready to hand, forget how idle they have been hitherto. But the thoughts of a despairing man reply with nothing but a medley of ideas, which he cannot disentangle; a hundred and one voices seem to answer, each stammering at first and then suddenly breaking off altogether, till all are silenced, and only the old question remains—

"What shall I do?"

For a long while Lucas sat thus in the attic, the tormenting query ringing in his ears. At last he shook himself, and thrusting his thoughts impatiently from him, took refuge in the last stronghold of those who can see no escape from their distress. He began to dream. One day a rich man would come to him and say: "Would you like to go to Italy to learn some noble craft? Good, my son, here are ten ducats. They will enable you to travel free from care. There is enough there to take you to Florence and even further. Take the money and think no more about it; it is nothing to me. Often I stake ten ducats on a card and lose as much five or ten times over in an evening without feeling it. How many times have I given a girl ten ducats for a smile? Look at the buckle on my shoe; it is worth thirty ducats, and yet I was not put out for a moment when one of them was stolen."

Surely, mused Lucas, as he continued to weave daydreams, there must be many good men in the world. Father often used to say there were, and I think he was right. But how strange it is that one should have to go down on one's knees to good men before they will do anything! If they are good, surely they must know that others are dying of hunger and thirst! And they must know that for a trifle, for the price of a shoebuckle, a man can often be saved. Is it kindness to give alms to the beggar at the church door? Even with the money in his hand, he still remains a beggar. There must be hundreds and hundreds of good men in the world, and if the beggar is to earn his daily bread, many of them must pass by and put a copper in his hand. Yet they do not save him from having to beg! But he would never have become a beggar if he had been helped. Perhaps the most terrible thing on earth is that men do not hold out a helping hand to one another.

Attracted by the broad expanse of sky which seemed to stretch above it, he walked to the window. It was a small attic window, and to reach it he had to climb up two rough wooden steps. He leaned on the broad sill and gazed happily at the glorious view stretching beneath him far away to the horizon. At his feet he could see the dark foliage of the trees on the bastion; in front of the walls lay the broad green expanse of the glacis, intersected by streets and paths that looked like streaks of chalk. Beyond came the houses, roofs and church-towers of the suburbs, and yet further away, the hills rose gently to the diaphanous mist of the mountains.

With one swift, all-embracing glance Lucas took in the view. Along the broad highway which crossed the glacis in the direction of the suburbs, a long procession was advancing at a fair pace, looking like some giant caterpillar with arching back crawling along on its myriad feet. At first Lucas watched it quite unmoved, but suddenly he saw that it was the same procession he had met a little while back in the square in front of

St. Michael's Church. He grew wildly excited. Although it was a long way off, he could plainly discern the cuirassiers riding ahead. As the light played about the cavalcade and sudden gleams flashed on bright points on their helmets, they were clearly distinguishable. Yes, there were the traveling coaches, like crawling black beetles. Behind them came another troop of horsemen.

Lucas kept his eyes fixed on the procession. It formed a whole community making its exodus. Advancing in close array, it constituted a single whole that had cut itself adrift from the town and left behind it all those who must remain rooted to the place. Far away in the distance, further than eye could see, in a foreign land, lay the goal that lured it on. Night and day it would march forward until at last it reached that goal and was swallowed up in its wide embrace. Lucas gazed into the distance. His eyes felt an irresistible impulse to follow the procession. He could visualize the whole journey. His heart began to beat furiously. "Oh how lucky they are!" he sighed. "How lucky they are!"

Then, remembering the beautiful dog he had seen

running by the side of the Archduke's carriage, he banged his fist down on the window-sill. "Oh God!" he raged, "I envy even that dog!" At each word, he thumped the window-sill. "If only I could go with them—with them!" Then, seized by a sudden inspiration, he added: "If I were allowed to be myself every other day, only every other day, I wouldn't mind a bit. . . . I shouldn't mind being that dog if I could go with them on their journey. . . ."

Whereupon in the twinkling of an eye he found he was a dog running along by the side of the Archduke's coach.

When he struck the window-sill with his fist, Lucas had not noticed that there was a ruddy-looking metal ring sunk into the dirty old wood-work. Indeed, in his excitement, he was quite unconscious of the violent movements of his hand. How was he to know that the thin yellow hoop which cut a circle in the wood, was of pure gold? How was he to guess that the spot where it was imbedded possessed the virtue of fulfilling for anyone a wish expressed while his hand lay on the magic circle? Lucas had spoken and, without knowing it, he had brought down his fist inside the magic circle with every word he uttered. And thus the miracle had taken place! All he had felt was a sort of giddiness seizing him as he uttered the last words; everything had reeled before his eyes, as if he were falling into a deep swoon. A violent blow had struck him and taken away his breath. Everything had happened in a flash.

I must be dreaming, he thought, as he bounded along beside the Archduke's coach. He was conscious that the dog's body was his own, and though he could hardly believe it, he was pleasantly surprised. He marveled that he could run along on four legs, and thought it a great joke. Yet he was amazed to find it quite natural and comfortable. Numberless scents, of which he had never before been aware, filled the air on every side, and he felt an irresistible longing to sniff them out and find whither they led. He was conscious of the rattling of wheels all around him, a confusion of voices, and the clatter of a hundred horses' hooves, like the beating of hailstones in a storm. His thoughts were turbid, yet entirely alert and wakeful.

I'm dreaming, he thought. I'm dreaming a wonderful dream.

Then for a moment he was overcome with a feeling of unnameable horror. He tried to cry out, but all he heard was a bark. Whereupon his terror turned to such wonderful good cheer, that he was forced to laugh. But his laugh too sounded like a rather shrill, quivering bark, and in uttering it he could not resist the impulse to throw his head up. At the same moment, he saw above him the Archduke's pale face leaning forward and looking down at him through the crystal window of the coach. He felt rather frightened, and quickly dropped his head again.

What a mad dream.

His limbs were filled with a desire to spring and jump about, and he bounded forward lightly at a pace that delighted him. In a moment he had raced ahead of the coach-horses.

What a dream! he thought again.

I wonder whether I could run off into the fields?

"Cambyses!"

He stopped short. At once he knew that the call was meant for him. He knew it was his name and felt an irresistible impulse, an overpowering readiness to obey. Turning round he ran back to the coach.

"Cambyses!"

It was the voice of one of the lackeys standing on the tailboard. Lucas looked back at the man, and heard him add: "That's right. . . . Good dog! . . . Stay here!"

And then they went on.

He felt he would like to obtain a closer view of the Archduke. And raising his head again and again, he looked up at the window of the coach. His efforts must have attracted attention, for a few words caught his pricked-up ears. In his anxiety to understand what was being said, he forgot to observe that even in his efforts to listen, his body responded to his will exactly like that of a dog, and that all unconsciously he felt impeled to prick up or drop his ears. He now heard words of command issuing from the interior; one of the lackeys raised his hand to warn the procession in the rear, and the coach suddenly halted. The door was opened and the Archduke leaned forward slightly toward the dog.

"Well, Cambyses . . . already tired of running, are you?"

The words were uttered in a stern, sharp voice, only artificially softened by a friendliness both labored and unfamiliar.

With feelings of mingled fear and joy Lucas looked up into the arrogant face peering down on him. He tried to reply, to utter a greeting, but was aware that every effort at expression made by his will merely ran down his back. He tried to be friendly and to smile, but even these desires ran down his back and became active somewhere there. Springing aside, he turned his head. Behind him he felt something unfamiliar moving, signifying his answer, his greeting and his smile. Lo and behold! he discovered that he was wagging his tail!

"He can lie on the floor inside if he's tired," he heard the Archduke say, close above his head, addressing a gentleman sitting opposite him, his back to the horses;

"after all, he can't be expected to run the whole of the journey." And, without waiting for an answer, he again leaned out, threw the door wide open, and called out: "Well, Cambyses—jump up!"

I shall never be able to do that! thought Lucas, dropping his shoulders and scratching the dust with his forepaws, as he measured the height of the coach. He wanted to thank the Archduke effusively and beg him to wait a moment. As he did so, he noticed that his tail was wagging more and more violently.

"Come along, jump up!" The Archduke's tone was sharper. The words seemed to lift Lucas from the ground and hurl him up. He jumped, feeling as light as a feather, and in a trice was standing on the mat of the coach. The door closed with a bang.

"Lie down!"

Lucas collapsed at the feet of his master as though he had been struck by lightning. Before him he could see only the dainty little shoes, with their glittering diamond buckles and red heels that shone like blood, while his nose could scent the delicate aromas exhaled by the

Archduke's silk stockings, his furs and his clothes.

Swaying gently from side to side, the coach drove on. He could hear the dull rolling of the wheels, the snorting of the horses, and the faint jumble of murmuring voices.

After a while he raised himself up cautiously and sat on his haunches, examining the Archduke more closely with eager curiosity. He saw his thin proud face, his pallid cheeks, his large bright eyes, gazing apathetically and superciliously into the distance, his hard mouth, always slightly open beneath his long refined nose, and his lower lip protruding as if in disdain. The listless face, with its expression of imperious and unquestioned authority, filled him with astonishment and fascinated him as an altogether new phenomenon.

By way of comparison he cast a swift glance at the man on the seat opposite. He had a round, contented face, of a type sufficiently common, somewhat somnolent and at the same time alert, ever on the *qui vive* for a sudden word of command. Quickly Lucas turned to look at the Archduke again.

"What do you want now, Cambyses?"

Lucas felt his body quiver at the sound of this voice. But he continued to study his master's face with passionate, searching curiosity.

For a moment or two the pair of them, the man and the dog, remained looking into each other's eyes. Then suddenly the smile that touched the Archduke's lips vanished, his face clouded over, and a faint trace of embarrassment suffused his pale cheeks.

"Stop that, Cambyses! Don't stare like that!" Heaving a sigh he fell back in his seat. "Strange," he observed to the gentleman-in-waiting opposite him, who leaned forward eagerly to catch his words, "strange how a dog like that sometimes has a look that is quite human . . . as if he wanted to say something. . . . I don't mean to be rude, Waltersburg, but just then Cambyses looked more intelligent than you do."

At midnight Lucas woke up with a start. Gradually he became aware that he was lying on the ground, covered in straw. A moist heat, soft as a blanket, enveloped him and with every breath he inhaled the pungent smell of sweating horses. He could hear the jangling of chains, and snorting and bellowing; the occasional stamp of hooves fell vaguely on his ears. Timidly he raised his head. Close beside him stood an animal which, seen from below in the dim ruddy glow of a lantern, seemed to loom up like a giant. Lucas sprang to his feet in horror. He was in a stable! Close beside him the magnificent white horse at whose feet he had been sleeping began to stir, and then he saw all the six great white horses that had drawn the Archduke's coach on the previous day. There they stood side by side, separated only by low partitions. He recognized them at once, their white backs gleaming brightly above the dark boards at their sides. Their gorgeous harness was hanging on pegs high up on the wall.

Utterly dumbfounded, Lucas staggered forward, rubbing his eyes and trying to remember what had happened. But his mind was a blank and, overcome by terror that increased every moment, he let his hand drop to his side, and stared about him, wondering whether he could not possibly escape from his strange surroundings. His anxious eyes suddenly caught sight of the stable door. Trembling all over, he crept breathless, step by step, toward it. Gently he raised the latch and paused for a moment, in case one of the grooms who might be sleeping in the stables should wake up. Then, cautiously opening the heavy door which creaked discordantly on its hinges, he slipped like lightning through the opening. He was free.

Not until he felt the cold night wind on his face did he really wake up. Then fear clutched at his heart with redoubled intensity, and he trembled so violently that he could hardly breathe. Pulling himself together, he began to run. His terror seemed to hang like a weight about his limbs, his feet felt like lead, and yet his fear lashed him on. In the dim light of the waning moon he could see the straggling houses of a small town. His footsteps rang like iron on the dry ground. Now and again a dog made a dash at him from behind a fence, a gate or a garden wall, and at the first sound of a bark, Lucas jumped as though shot. The bark echoed deep down into his heart, tearing away the veil which sleep had drawn across his memory, suddenly revealing ghostlike pictures of experiences which, at once confused yet terribly distinct, merged into one another.

On gaining the open highway, he ran without heeding his direction and continued until his strength gave out. He rested a moment, then walked on as fast as he could, on and on, until he was able to run again; and not until his knees felt like giving way beneath him did he stop. Walking and running alternately he reached at early dawn a slight elevation, on which was a stone monument called the Spinnerin am Kreuz. From this he knew that he was on the Wienerberg, and had not mistaken the way home. Here he took a short rest in order to recover his breath. He could see the walls of the city in the distance, the church towers below emerging from the darkness of the night; while beyond were the mountains looming through the morning mist. Overcome with emotion, he pondered over the power that had conducted him thus far afield.

Presently he started to walk slowly down the road.

He was worn out by his long run and a prey to the fears that surged afresh in his breast every moment, and dazed by the mystery which he could not explain. When at last he reached the house on the bastion, it was broad daylight and the streets were already full of life. Creeping up the stairs to the attic, he flung himself on the bed to rest. But, as he could not sleep, he soon got up again, hurried downstairs, and timidly strolled about. The sing-song of the street-hawkers, the hurrying crowd, and the rattle of the traffic helped him to forget his state of painful wonder and to feel at one with everyday life. It comforted him to feel his fellow-creatures all about him; he had a sensation of security when he heard them talking or saw them laughing.

Quite unconsciously he turned down the road leading to the Imperial Palace, and, taking up his stand on the square in front of St. Michael's Church, waited, as though he expected the pageant of yesterday to be re-enacted. But nothing of the sort happened. The square wore its usual aspect, people crossed and re-crossed in all directions, no fence of halberds barred their path, and the Palace, with its old gray walls, stood out calm and massive as a lonely promontory. In his bewilderment Lucas had cherished a confused hope that in this square, where all his adventures of the previous day had started, he would find a solution, or at least the suggestion of an answer to the riddle of what had happened. But with a sudden feeling of profound disappointment, he walked crestfallen away. It then chanced to occur to him that some of his father's friends were at work nearby on the Palace which the Papal Nuncio was having built for himself. Overcome by an overpowering longing for company, he hastened on in the hope of finding them.

Passing through the courtyard, he entered the new structure through a door made of rough boards, and immediately found himself surrounded by a din of hammering, blow after blow raining down on the stones, the shriek of saws, the screech of files, and the songs with which the workmen beguiled their labors. They were all Italians—sculptors, stonemasons, and iron-workers—they sang Italian songs, which Lucas had

often enough heard his father sing. Amid the cheerful buzz of work, swelled and lightened by the singing which perforce banished superfluous care and
unprofitable thought, all Lucas's fears and dark fore-
bodings melted away.

He immediately felt at home in this environment.
As a little boy, he had played by his father's side in just
such building-yards as this, mixing with the other men,
all of whom knew him. Maestro Andrea Chini, who
was working with his assistants, understood without
being told that poverty alone was forcing young Lucas
Grassi to descend to work that was beneath him, and
he proceeded to find what light jobs he could for him.
That day Lucas accepted the work eagerly, with none
of the feelings of reluctance he had experienced before,
and performed his duties cheerfully. As for all the hopes
and longings he had so ardently cherished only the day
before, he refused to give them another thought, and
put them out of his mind as over-ambitious. After all
the mysterious events that had occurred, he felt that he
should do penance for his arrogant aspirations. By the

time he had received friendly greetings from all and sundry, and had unwittingly taken his share in their conversation and even joined in snatches of their songs, he had ceased to brood over what had happened. He even began to doubt whether it were true. Tired out, but with his mind at rest, he returned home in the evening with the comforting feeling that he had escaped from some danger, or from the meshes of a strange delusion. He fell asleep immediately.

Suddenly he was awakened by a kick which seemed to go right through his body, and found himself lying on the ground. Above him was the broad red face of a fat footman in livery, who was on the point of kicking him again.

"Hullo, here's Cambyses back again!" shouted the man. "Get up, you rascal. Where the devil have you been all day?"

Lucas sprang to his feet in horror. Yes, he was back in a stable again, the doors stood wide open, the morning light was pouring in, and the men were leading the fine white horses out one by one, already harnessed. As Lucas tried to escape another kick, the fat man caught hold of him by the scruff of the neck, just behind his ears.

"Hi, you lout!" he called out, "just hand me a bit of rope, so that I sha'n't lose the brute again!"

The grooms and stable-boys all laughed.

"You don't want a bit of rope, Master Pointner," said one of them. "Cambyses won't run away. If he had wanted to run away, he wouldn't have come back at all."

"Really!" retorted the fat man angrily. "And what about yesterday? Where was the rascal all day yesterday, I'd like to know?"

"With one of his sweethearts, I expect," replied another of the grooms, and all the stable-hands roared with laughter. Meanwhile a young groom called Caspar had come up, a gentle, handsome boy with an amiable face.

"Please don't be so hard on Cambyses, Master Pointner," he begged, "or one of these fine days he'll go off for good. I assure you, sir, it would be much better to

stroke him and make a fuss of him. Believe me, I understand dogs, as you know. Just think how clever it was
of him to find us. How he must have run to catch up
with us, and how nicely he has taken to his proper place
again. You may take my word for it, Master Pointner,
that dog's run the deuce of a long way just to get back
to us. . . . Good old Cambyses, good dog! . . . Let him go,
Master Pointner. . . ."

Pointner withdrew his hand, and the young groom
smiled again. "Just look at him," he said. "That dog understands every blessed word! Look how he's turning from
me to you and you to me. . . . Yes, good old Cambyses,
good dog, come along! . . ." And leaning forward, he
stroked the dog's back and patted him kindly on the
breast, between his forelegs, as men fondle horses.

"There, just see how pleased he is," he observed with
a laugh, as he drew himself up. "There's no need for a
rope. Just call him kindly to you, and he'll follow, and
our gracious lord will be overjoyed that the dog is back
again."

"Come along!" cried the fat man sullenly and left

the stable. "Come along, you sly rascal . . . !" And Lucas followed to heel.

The Archduke was sitting at breakfast with various gentlemen of his suite, when his Groom-of-the-Chamber entered. The dog behind him sprang into the room.

"Your Grace, the dog has come back!" said Pointner.

"Oh ho!" cried the Prince with a laugh. "Cambyses, come here! Where did you find him, Dietrich?"

"Lying in the stable as usual," Pointner replied sullenly. "The rascal was sleeping as if nothing had happened."

The Archduke shrugged his shoulders. "Oh well, so long as he's back! Don't you ever run away from me again, you vagabond!" he added, leaning forward and addressing the dog under the table. All the courtiers laughed.

But on the following day the dog disappeared again.

This time Lucas wandered about the woods on the snow-clad hills, in country that was quite strange to him. He made no attempt to return to Vienna, for it was clear that the city must now be too far away, and that it would be impossible for him to reach it from this hilly country in a day's march. Moreover, he was beginning to see the futility of trying to escape. He set to work carefully to recapitulate all that had happened, and reach some decision which would enable him to face with greater confidence whatever the future held in store. But his fears constantly got the better of him. Twice he had scoured the countryside as a dog, and he knew by now, with all his senses fully awake, that it had been no dream. He had been lured away, over hill and down dale, away from the city to which it was impossible for him now to return. And he must perforce continue the journey. There had been a time when this had been the darling wish of his heart. In fact it was only three days ago, but now it seemed to be ages back, lost in the mists of time. And lo! his wish had been fulfilled so that it seemed nothing but a bitter mockery; it had been granted in such an unmerciful way as to debase him. He was harnessed to the life of a dog, forced to follow its tracks, and shivering with cold and trembling with hunger, was compelled to creep along whatever road the dog chose to take.

Toward nightfall Lucas was standing on the top of the hill looking on the lights beginning to twinkle in the little town far down below at his feet. Utterly exhausted, he remained rooted to the spot. It grew darker and darker. Presently, sitting down in the snow, he counted the chimes as they rang out from the church towers in the valley, and with resigned but breathless curiosity, awaited the transformation. It took place at midnight. He only just had time to hear the first stroke of the hour, when he felt a sudden shock, similar to the one he had experienced before, when he had been standing at his attic window. It fell on him before he could draw a single breath; he thought the ground was opening beneath his feet. Just as he imagined he was taking leave of his senses, he felt himself being violently whisked away. And the next moment he was once more lying in warm straw, his sharpened olfactory nerves became aware of the scent of hay about him, and the smell of sweating horses in the stable, while a church clock close by rang out the hour of midnight—eleven strokes! But it was a different chime from the one that had struck the first stroke he had heard. It sounded deeper.

The following morning Caspar, the young groom, shook him gently to wake him, and, after feeding him, took him at once to the Archduke's Groom-to-the-Chamber.

"Well, Cambyses, where have you been again?" Caspar enquired, laughing good-naturedly as he led him along. "Where have you been, Cambyses?" he repeated again and again. They crossed the courtyard of a Palace, ascended a flight of stately marble steps, and entered a dark paneled hall full of servants busy making all manner of preparations, while the Groom-of-the-Chamber stood by issuing his orders to them and picking his teeth.

"Master Pointner," cried Caspar from the doorway, "Cambyses has come back all right."

Pointner ceased giving orders and picking his teeth. He looked sullenly at the dog who had leaped into the room and at the groom who had remained standing at the door.

"Just come back?" he enquired.

"No," replied Caspar, "he was lying in the stable and had slept there all night."

The Archduke, wearing a loose fur cloak, was warming himself by the fire in a luxurious apartment. Count Waltersburg was standing in front of him. As soon as the latter caught sight of the Groom-of-the-Chamber coming in with the dog he went into fits of laughter. "There's that rascal back again after all, and your Imperial Highness thought it impossible for the dog to run all that way over the hills."

The Archduke looked down at Cambyses, who had quietly stretched himself in front of the fire. "Yes indeed! And he seems all right. Well, I'm very glad. I was afraid he might have been frozen to death." He gave the dog a sly dig in the ribs with the point of his shoe.

Count Waltersburg shook his head. "A good thrashing would be the best thing," he observed thoughtfully. "Otherwise the brute will think he can run away and come back again just as he pleases."

The Archduke cast an enquiring glance up at Pointner,

who shrugged his shoulders peevishly. "It might be just as well," he said.

"Well then," commanded the Archduke, "go ahead with it." At these words the dog sprang to his feet looking in alarm from one to the other.

"Amazing!" laughed Waltersburg. "Anyone would think he understood every word." The dog gave him a penetrating, imploring look, but Waltersburg only laughed the louder. "Yes, dear friend, it's no good looking like that. You've got to be punished."

"Cambyses!" called Pointner sternly, turning toward the door.

"Where are you going?" the Archduke enquired.

"I thought it would be better to do it outside," stammered Pointner.

"No, here!" was the Archduke's cold and curt command.

Pointner still hesitated and then began slowly and reluctantly to unfasten the belt about his portly belly.

"Are you going to do it today or tomorrow," cried the Archduke.

The first blow crashed down. The dog fell flat on the floor and howled. The second blow was a miss, but in his terror the dog howled more loudly than ever. The third and fourth blows did not strike him square, but were very painful notwithstanding.

"Give it to me, Dietrich!" exclaimed the Archduke. "You're no good! You hit too fast and too irregularly. Give it to me, Dietrich!" He spoke in short gasps, and his hollow cheeks were slightly flushed. Seizing the belt impatiently and leaning forward in his armchair, he raised his arm and slowly let blow after blow fall. His aim was sure and he hit hard. The dog writhed frantically under the blows, his howl rising to a shriek of despair, a heart-rending wail. But the belt whizzed down on him faster and faster, whistling as it cleaved the air. The dog made one faint attempt to get up and escape, but collapsed all of a heap under the hail of blows, and his howling died down as if drowned in tears. The Archduke was in a frenzy, and took no notice of Pointner.

"Your Grace, please!" exclaimed the man anxiously.

But the Archduke might have been drunk as he continued swinging the belt and panting with ever-increasing fury.

"There! There! There!" he cried in hoarse, almost inaudible tones, wellnigh beside himself with rage. Suddenly his arm dropped and he fell back in his chair. His head drooped forward; he was white as death and choked and gasped for breath; his eyes rolled.

Clumsy and fat as he was, Pointner darted like lightning to a ewer of water, plunged a cloth into it and bathed the Archduke's brow.

"Run across the road for the doctor!" he growled in fierce fury at Waltersburg, who was standing by horrified, not knowing what to do. "Could you think of nothing better to do than persuade him to thrash that dog? What? Have you forgotten how dangerous it is to put him up to such pranks, or are you an absolute fool? Quick! Run for the doctor! At least do as you are bid!"

Waltersburg fled from the room.

The dog lay motionless on the floor.

· · ·

Lucas stood in the middle of the highway. In the distance, on a little hill beyond which a wall of mountains
towered like snow-clad battlements, the castle in which
he had been thrashed the day before shimmered faintly
in the first rays of dawn. On the human body, to which
he had returned once more, he could feel the wounds
the dog had received, while his memory still smarted
with a sensation of burning resentment against the
fright, the pain and the bloody disgrace to which he
had been subjected.

"What has happened to me?" he groaned aloud.
"What has happened to me?" he repeated wildly again
and again, with a faint sigh of despair.

How could he guess that the spell which lay upon
him every other day obliterated alternately the form
of Lucas and that of the dog? How could he possibly
know that all that had been left to him was his human
mind, that intangible basic entity which is able to say
"I," but that nevertheless he was forced every other day
to adopt all the physical attributes and habits of the
dog, and that this was bound to go on until the spell

was broken? As long as the Archduke and his retinue remained in Florence, the lives of the young man Lucas and of the dog Cambyses had to be merged in one, and could not be on earth together at the same time. The "I" of Cambyses had been whisked away to some obscure corner of the universe, where it hung invisibly suspended, sunk in the deepest slumber and possibly seeing in its dreams vague far-away reflections of the experiences its absent body was undergoing. In uttering his wish Lucas had declared that he would not mind being a dog every other day; and so the body of a dog had been given him. But as soon as the Archduke left Florence for the north, whither Lucas felt no yearning to go, the latter would be free and the real Cambyses would once more be running beside the traveling coach drawn by its six white horses.

But for the time being Lucas, overcome with horror and despair, knew nothing of all this.

One by one the snow-clad peaks became suffused with a soft roseate glow. Broad red-gold rays poured down into the valley, cutting through the mist like giant swords, while the castle battlements gleamed in tongues of flame as the sun rose on the horizon.

As if the light of day had brought home to him more acute than ever his solitary, unhappy plight, Lucas suddenly flung himself violently on the cold ground and, burying his head in his arms, sobbed aloud.

"Who's that crying there like a little child . . . ?"

The words were spoken in a deep gruff voice just above Lucas's head, and a hand shook him roughly by the shoulder. "Who is it, crying like that?" The gruff voice spoke more gently. "There . . . there . . ." it said kindly. "Hush . . . hush!"

Lucas slowly arose.

Before him stood an old man with a wild gray beard, hollow cheeks, ruddy from the chill morning air, and a pair of lively, laughing little eyes. He was a dear old fellow, not very tall, but sturdily built and youthful in his bearing.

He pulled his little knapsack around and began fumbling with it, while his sharp, inquisitive eyes scrutinized Lucas's features intently.

Then he averted his gaze and observed quite simply, as though he had just been interrupted in a long conversation, "Hadn't we better sit down? . . . I think that would be the best thing to do . . ."

So saying, he sat down on the bank by the side of the road, resting his knapsack on his knees. As Lucas still hesitated, he smiled and beckoned to him, till at last he persuaded him to take a seat beside him. And thus they sat side by side for a while. The old man dived into his knapsack and produced a piece of bread and some bacon rind, together with a bottle of liquor. He drank, cut the bread and the bacon and handed Lucas some of it from time to time, though he avoided looking at him as he did so.

Lucas accepted the food and ate it. The old man then handed him the bottle over his shoulder. This too Lucas took, and a strong pull of brandy sent a glow all through his body.

"Yes," observed the old man, as though he were talking to himself, "it's a fine world . . . a great big world. . . . How glorious it is over there . . . beautiful mountains and a lovely valley. . . . But can one stop rooted to one spot? . . .

No, a call comes to us all . . . a call that rings ceaselessly in our ears!"

He was silent for a while.

"I have remained rooted to one spot long enough," he continued, "my whole life, in fact. More than once I heard the call in the distance. But I thought to myself . . . call on, call on! . . . there's plenty of time. . . . And I stayed where I was . . . always in the same spot until I grew old and gray . . . that was surely long enough!"

The words were uttered with eager animation, as though he were in the middle of a long and exciting discussion, instead of having only just opened his mouth to say all he had to say. His active mind worked quickly, and his tone of voice made it plain that he was firmly convinced he was right.

"People came in and out of my place," he continued, "people I knew and people I didn't know. They came across the Wenzel bridge, from the Altstadt over to the Kleinseite . . . and they came to me. . . . Yes, and it was never too far for them to come . . . when they wanted clothes, a doublet at once, or a pair of breeches by the morning . . . or a new coat for Easter Sunday . . . then they came fast enough . . . yes, and they went swaggering round the town in the fine clothes I made for them, or danced about in their luxurious homes . . . or else they went and rolled themselves in mud and shame somewhere. God knows where they all paraded themselves in their finery! Many of them went out into the wide, wide world. . . . Many of them drove up in their coaches to my house and waited, stamping and cursing, while the last stitches were being put in. Then they would snatch the coat out of my hands, fling the money in my face, and get back to their carriages in a flash . . . and away! And up and away . . . into the wide, wide world!"

He laughed, spat and drank.

"People tell you all sorts of things," he went on. "They say that where the land ends the sea begins. Yes! You stand on the beach and look out, and there is nothing but water. Only sky and water! And that is the sea . . . the sea. . . ." He almost chanted the word.

"Yes and then . . ." and he wrenched himself from the subject of the sea with a sort of jerk. "Yes, and then they say there is a country where it is never cold, where it never snows, and there is no winter. Only spring and summer. Always sunshine . . . always sunshine. . . ."

"Yes!" cried Lucas.

The old man turned toward him. His expression, at once quizzical and encouraging, warmed Lucas's heart.

"Yes?" repeated the old fellow with a note of enquiry. "No winter . . . always spring and summer? And what about the sea? Always water and sky? The sea . . ." he chanted. "Well, He has done some strange things," he added, pointing up to the sky. "What a jumble of a world He has made!"

He chuckled to himself as though he had cracked a joke.

"And He has made a jumble of men too . . . eh? Now I say 'water,' don't I? And you say 'water,' don't you? So you see . . . but there are people who say 'eau' . . . do you follow? And others who say 'aqua'—and at home, where I come from, where they all live huddled together cheek by jowl, some say 'water' like you and me, but others say 'wodu'. . . . Silly, isn't it? Yes. He wouldn't allow anybody to take liberties with Him!" He wagged his head. "Oh, the idiots, what fools they made of themselves with their old tower! They wanted to build right up to Him, right to His very door . . . and be able to go in and out of His house, without even knocking, as if He were a fellow workman or an old chum. . . ."

The old man spoke emphatically, as though it had all happened only yesterday.

"The fools!" he exclaimed. "Surely they ought to have known from the start that He wouldn't stand that sort of thing! But no—and then all of a sudden, there they were, one saying 'water,' another 'aqua,' and a third 'wodu'—and Heaven knows what else! And then, of course, it was all up with their fine tower. . . ."

He laughed. And lying stretched out on the edge of the road, supporting his head on his hands, he gazed into the distance and fell into silent meditation. Lucas sat beside him without saying a word.

"Yes," observed the old fellow after a while, wagging his head and speaking with great deliberation, "not only was it all up with the tower that day . . . but also with any idea of men ever working together again. In those days mankind was still an actuality . . . men still understood one another . . . and they tried to produce a great work together . . . a piece of idiocy. . . . They might have thought of something better. . . . But they were at least united. Ever since that day, however, they have never been united . . . they can never be united again. . . . Ever since one said this and t'other said that, so that neither understood the other, all who say 'water' stick together, and the man who says 'aqua' sticks to the chap who says 'aqua' like he does. Yes, and ever since that day there have been only men, but no mankind. . . ."

Lucas listened, but did not understand what the old man was talking about. The one point he grasped was that even this old fellow beside him spoke of mysteries and miracles.

"But no!" ejaculated the old man once more, as if somebody had just contradicted him. "He need not have punished them so severely as all that! What would have happened if they had finished their wretched tower, eh? What then? Just imagine—there stands the tower, just try to picture it in your mind's eye . . . and from its top story you can step straight into His Parlour. . . . Well, what then? Suppose one of them had set out as a child and made up his mind to get up to Him . . . well? He would have climbed and climbed up the tower all his life . . . and done nothing else, done no work, and neither friend nor wife could have held him back. He would have climbed ever higher and higher . . . and the years would have rolled by, and still he would not have got so very far toward his goal. . . . And he would have grown old and weary, but still he would have been nearer to earth than to heaven . . . and then he would have died . . . died on the way, remained lying there, before he had reached the top. Do you see? But He always punishes straight away . . . and punishes severely. . . . Yes. . . . Though perhaps He may be over-hasty when we make Him angry."

He shrugged his shoulders and laughed again. "As far as I am concerned, the tower might have been standing there forever and a day. . . . I should never have climbed its steps. . . . I have managed to remain all my life rooted to one spot, and I should have stuck there. . . . I should have stuck there quite content . . . for what would have been the good? . . . Things were all right as they were. . . . But then I used to hear people talking about a country where there was no winter, a country of lofty mountains where, even in the hottest summer, the snow never melted . . . and I heard them talking about the sea. . . ."

He turned and looked at Lucas, his curly beard making his wizened face appear aflame with animation, while his sharp, merry eyes twinkled with laughter.

"I waited until my wife grew old and my son was a settled man. What can one do with an old wife? And what is there to do in the nursery when one's son is grown up and settled down in life? Well then! The time had come. And so I left. Now it's for the boy to sit and make clothes; he knows all about it; he learned it all with me. It was no use saying, 'Father, stay with us!' or weeping and wailing, 'Don't go away!' That was all nonsense. They could snivel as much as they liked. I turned a deaf ear. When things are done, they're done! Just try telling a burned-out stove to give out more heat, as you want to cook some more soup and stew some more apples on it ... just you try.... The fire is out and the stove is cold and you can go on talking till you're black in the face."

He gave a loud merry laugh. "But I must be up and off, on and on until I reach the country where there is no winter ... for I want to convince myself once and for all of its existence. I want to go on and on until I reach the sea. You know ... you stand on the beach like this ... and over yonder there's nothing but sky and sea.... The sea ... I want to look on that with my own eyes now ... I must see that ... !"

And rising hurriedly to his feet, he threw his knapsack over his shoulder. Lucas went with him. The old man went uphill along the road. After a while he began to sing.

And thus they went on together, Lucas feeling happy in the old man's company. He tried to remember how long he had been alone, because hitherto he had kept out of the way of men when he was allowed to wander about in his own human form. And he recollected that recently he had always been a dog when in the presence of men.

The old man talked, sang, or whistled all the time. "Always snow," he observed, "always cold, so cold that your fingers grow stiff. How long have I been on the road now? . . . It's just possible that it's all a hoax. But we shall see. . . . I am curious, and I shall walk and walk as long as there's a road for me to walk on. They won't catch me getting tired . . . so they needn't think it . . . not me!" And he laughed and began to whistle again.

Lucas trudged along in silence by his side; the old fellow expected no reply nor did he ask for one. But that evening as they were sitting together on the edge of a wood, and saw the houses of a little town nestling deep in the snow before them, Lucas began to talk. The whole mystery which had, as it were, cut his life in two, and cast it out into the world in two halves, the strangeness of it, which took his breath away and frightened him out of his wits—he poured it all out, shy and stammering at first, but gradually with greater vehemence and emphasis, as though he were crying aloud for help.

The old man listened calmly; the tale did not seem to surprise him in the least. "But what does it matter?" he exclaimed, when Lucas's voice at last died away in sobs. "What does it matter? Why cry about it? Nonsense! Look on and marvel—that's the thing! Look on and wait—that's all! What are you grizzling about? Have you had an accident? Have they cut off your head or amputated one of your legs? Well then! And aren't you making your way to the place you want to get to? Why lose heart? Just look on, my dear child, just look on! Today you must wonder what is going to happen tomorrow, and tomorrow what is going to happen the day after . . . and so the time flies. If a man isn't inquisitive, there's no interest left in life."

And he sang softly to himself.

It began to get dark; one or two lights twinkled at them from the windows of the houses in the distance. He stood up and walked forward in the direction of the town.

Lucas was left alone.

• • •

From that day on Lucas bore his fate with ever-increasing fortitude. He began casting his thoughts ahead into the future; he sent them forward, across hill and dale, into the country he was approaching.

And he felt himself drawing ever closer to that country. All the roads now ran downhill; they presented no difficulties and were pleasant to walk along. A gentle zephyr filled the air with the breath of good tidings. Green meadows stretched out for miles around, fruit trees in blossom adorned the gentle slopes of the hills, while the box and laurel with their festoons of drooping wistaria stood out dark green about the white garden walls. A fragrance, strong yet subtle, such as he had never known before, seemed to exhale from the very earth itself, or to be wafted down from heaven on the passing breeze. Even the sky seemed to be further above his head, a sheet of unbroken azure. All the heavy low-hanging clouds had almost imperceptibly vanished, while every day the sun grew brighter.

Lucas saw lizards, green as emeralds, glide swiftly away on the gleaming garden walls. They flashed across his path and burrowed into the white dust like colored darts of light. And a childhood memory that had long lain dormant suddenly leaped to life. Yes, he had seen these beautiful, nimble little creatures before, long, long ago. Gorgeous and gleaming they had darted past him then, too fast for him to catch. The whole picture came back to him; the white walls and the warm white dust of the roads, almost blinding in the sunlight. He felt certain that, as a child, he must have come this way. And lo and behold! he was returning, while above him stretched the blue canopy of the sky after which his heart had yearned so long.

He did not avoid his fellow-men now. In the little villages and towns which nestled in the bosom of the valleys, he would sit by the fountains, stroking the smooth white marble, basking in the sun, talking to the people. They spoke his father's language, and he felt that he knew every one of them. Often he would stop at some threshold, wanting nothing, anxious only to give the women and children a friendly greeting. If they looked mistrustfully at him, he would laugh or chaff them, and would get in return a laugh or a greeting which was more precious to him than gold. He strolled through the vineyards and lay on the edge of flower-strewn meadows, listening to the ceaseless buzzing of the bees.

Early one morning, when men and houses were still sunk in slumber, he was strolling along a wide open road through a village, when he caught sight of a girl walking some distance ahead of him. He could not help following because there was no other road through the village, and he was obliged to look at her as she was the only creature in the place who was up and about. She looked attractive; her gait was light and easy. She had caught the sound of his footsteps, but had cast only one swift glance back at him, and continued on her way. It was only when they were out on the main road at the end of the village that she stopped and began fumbling with a little bundle she was carrying.

Apparently she had done what she wanted by the time Lucas caught up with her. They smiled at each other, and continued on their way together in silence. Lucas was happy in her company. He did not notice that the girl's clothes were in rags, nor that her disheveled hair fell in a tangle about her brow and cheeks; all he knew was that her fresh little face, with its delicate mouth and soft dark-brown eyes, was made all the more fascinating by her wealth of curly locks and was agreeably complimented by the rosy skin of her dainty limbs and chest.

Silent and smiling they ascended the road to the woods side by side.

"Where do you come from?" Lucas enquired at last.

She shook her head, smiled, but said nothing.

He smiled back. "Where are you going?" he asked after a pause.

She shook her head as before.

Again Lucas waited. "Don't you wish to speak?" he asked, "or can't you? . . . Tell me, what do they call you?"

She looked kindly at him. "They call me Angelica . . . that's all."

As soon as they were in the wood, her eyes searched for a suitable resting-place, and she ran forward to an old, decayed tree-trunk on the ground, and perched herself upon it. Lucas sat down beside her. She was holding her little bundle in her lap; unfastening it, she produced some dried figs and some bread and cheese, rummaging about for them among a tangle of bright-colored bits of cloth, hair-combs, coins, and broken necklaces, and producing them as if by magic. In the medley there was even a rosary of juniper berries which had to be disentangled.

Lucas watched her closely. "Is all this yours?"

"This is all mine," she replied, changing the order and emphasis of the words, as though trying to improve on them, and gazing calmly at him the while.

He suppressed a smile. "Where did you get it all?" he asked, feigning surprise.

"Well, I've got it," was the reply, which sounded like a hint to ask no questions.

"I have nothing at all," observed Lucas, as if to himself.

She quietly offered him a piece of cheese and some figs, and they ate together.

When they had finished, she got up and they went on their way. The road led out of the wood and struck across fields and meadows, already bathed in warm sunshine. Angelica began to sing. Lucas listened in silence.

He thought he had heard the song before sung by the Italian workmen in Vienna.

"Join in, won't you?" she exclaimed, suddenly breaking off.

And so they sang together as they walked along side by side. After a while Lucas took her hand. It reminded him that since his father had led him along like this he had never walked hand in hand with anyone. He felt the girl's warm fingers clinging to his, and he sang more lustily than ever.

When they were tired they rested; sometimes they talked, but often they said nothing for long stretches at a time. Then they would jump up and walk on until they wanted to rest again. Once, as they were walking silently on in their sunlit desert solitude, they stopped, gazed into each other's eyes and kissed. Then they covered another long stretch of road, and stopped again. This time Lucas clasped her to his breast. He had never kissed a girl before. Gently releasing herself from his embrace, she shook her head, as if in remonstrance.

"Not yet . . . !" she whispered.

So they went on together again. The sun's rays poured fiercely down upon them, and the whole countryside was aflame in the life-giving light. "Now I no longer fear a dog's life!" cried Lucas, suddenly throwing up his arms with a sigh of relief.

"We all lead dogs' lives," she replied calmly. "So why be afraid of it? It is often hard, but sometimes it can be very fine. . . ."

In the evening, as the shadows fell about them, they sat together under the eaves of a deserted hut.

"I am alone too, quite alone," said Angelica in reply to the little that Lucas had told her about himself. "It is true I often have somebody with me. . . . How can I tell who it is? . . . But I am very lonely all the same. Sometimes I am glad when he leaves me again and I am really alone. Often I have taken to my heels and run away . . . but once . . . no, it was not good . . . I had someone with me, and then he left me alone . . . that was not good. . . ."

And shaking herself, she gave a soft low laugh. "So you have come all that way? I have come a long way too," she proceeded without waiting for a reply, "a very long way. . . . I was in Lugano . . . and then over there . . . somewhere quite different . . . Venice. . . . I have been everywhere. . . ."

And she leaned against his shoulder. "But you will stay with me now, won't you?"

"Always," replied Lucas.

"Tomorrow too?"

"Tomorrow . . . ?" His voice faltered. "Tomorrow I must go down there . . . into the . . . there's a town down there in the valley. . . ."

"I'll go with you."

"Impossible. . . ." He could hardly speak. "You mustn't come with me. . . . But the day after tomorrow I shall be free . . . and then we can meet again and keep together."

"Where?" she asked, in eager, incredulous tones, looking sadly at him.

"Just you say where," he entreated, "just tell me the exact spot and I'll be there, Angelica—I swear to you I'll be there. . . ."

"Well . . . in Rovereto . . . in front of the church."

"Very good, in Rovereto; but you must wait until I come."

"And you swear . . . ?"

"I swear. . . . But you swear too that you will wait."

She drew him to her and kissed him, and Lucas took her in his arms. He forgot the spell under which he was living, he forgot the time, the hours sped by, and he took no count of them.

Somewhere in the distance a church clock struck the hour of midnight. But Lucas did not hear it. All he knew was that a violent shock snatched him from Angelica's arms. He was utterly dazed and it was only later that he remembered the girl's horror when she suddenly found she was clasping nothing.

A few days later, Lucas, all aglow in the rays of the early morning sun, was standing on the last slope of the mountains. In the invisible depths of the valley at his feet the Adige went roaring on its way. He knew the river well, for had he not been following its winding course through wild gorges southward for the last week? Hidden by a mountain peak, it was close at hand, imprisoned in a rocky defile. He could hear it roaring and foaming, although from where he was standing, he could not see its final fight for freedom. But far away below, the spot where it entered the plain was visible. Still rushing and turbulent it spread in a broad stream over the land, but far away in the distance its waters became blue as the infinite heavens spreading above it.

Lucas stood on his hill, as though he were at the top of a tower. The valley lay peacefully spread out at his feet. He scanned it, drunk with joy—the soft pale-green fields, slashed here and there by white streaks of road, the gleaming silver inlay of the rushing streams, the whole shimmering and smiling brightly amid straggling homesteads and towns.

Immediately below, at no very great distance from the hills, and on the fringe of the plain which stretched as far as eye could see, gleamed the walls, roofs and towers of the city of Verona. Lucas felt as though he had but to spread his wings to float down to it. Never, during the whole of his journey, had he been filled with such impatience as he felt now. Down below there must surely be painters, sculptors and goldsmiths—men who would know all about Florence, about the masters who worked there and taught their craft, or about other places on Italian soil where such men could be found.

Close at hand, a little below the turf-clad hill on which he was sitting, he caught sight of a short stretch of road that looked like a piece of ribbon. Lower down it appeared again, winding down the incline, and unrolling across the green plain in a straight line.

It reminded him of his father who had traveled along that road in a northerly direction. It seemed to him incomprehensible that his father should have left this smiling garden, incredible that anyone who had been born and bred there could have forsaken such a glorious country.

All his hopes, desires and thoughts darted—nay, flew along that white ribbon unfolding far away in the distance across the green fields. He banished the memory of the day before yesterday, which stirred faintly in his breast. Afraid of meeting Angelica in front of the church of Rovereto, he had kept to sidetracks on the outskirts of the town and thus slipped by the little place unnoticed. Again and again he had felt tempted to go through the center of it straight to the church, to find out whether she were really waiting for him. But he did not think she was, for he felt sure she must be much too frightened to wish to find him; nevertheless, he longed for her beauty and her love, and he felt tormented by remorse for having so light-heartedly whiled away his time with her. He was certain that he had not only distressed her, but given her a terrible fright into the bargain. At last he had shaken himself free of all these thoughts—his longing, his remorse, his hesitation— and had gone on his way, thinking of nothing but his distant goal. And behold, he was now sitting on the edge of the plain, with no desire to think of anything else!

The sound of trotting horses, the rumble of carriage-wheels and the murmur of human voices drew ever nearer and nearer. On the strip of road that encircled the hill on which he was sitting, there appeared a troop of horsemen; a string of coaches followed, brought up

in the rear by another troop of horsemen. Lucas recognized the Archduke's cavalcade. It burst upon his
vision, with its horses and wagons, like actors appearing
on the stage, or mechanical figures within a clock, only
to disappear again, where a spur of the hill seemed to
swallow up the roadway. But the snorting of the horses,
the rattling of the chains, the screeching and groaning
of the wheels, and the confused murmur of voices filled
the air with life and animation.

Lucas sprang to his feet and breathlessly waited
until the procession once more came into view below.
And lo, down in the depths he could see it again, rattling downhill. Enveloped in clouds of dust, it glided
along as though borne on the bosom of the clouds.

"There! . . ." cried Lucas, throwing out his arms to it.
"There I am traveling to Verona! To-night I shall be in
Verona!"

The market-place of Verona was thronged with people.
On the cobblestones with which the square was paved,
all kinds of vegetables lay piled up in green mounds,

tangled masses of chickens tied by the feet cackled and squawked, the bleeding carcasses of bullocks, opened and cut up, gaped to view, while towering above it all a flaming mass of flowers and fruit rose in tier upon tier of gorgeous color.

The bright rays of the morning sun poured down on this medley of humanity, animals and vegetables. Everything was radiant, bright and warm. The air was full of the scent of flowers, raw meat, oranges and blood, clothes, stagnant water, wet metal, onions and melons. It vibrated with the shrill voices of the crowd, snatches of song, the shouting and crying of children as they played about, harsh discordant whistles, the braying of donkeys under the whip, and the cackling of tied-up chickens. The plashing of the fountain, the marble columns and statues, the lion of St. Mark, soaring above the tumult, the houses, the countless balconies, the flapping of blinds, and the fluttering of clothes hung out to dry at the windows—everything seemed to take a hand in the general commotion. The whole market-place was palpitating with life.

Lucas sauntered about, full of wonder and delight. All the turmoil seemed strange to him, but, at the same time, in the deepest recesses of his memory it was also familiar. He stopped by every group to try to hear what they were saying, and laughed happily when somebody caught him by the arm, offering him flowers, meat or whatnot for sale, asking him what he wanted, trying to discover his needs and his tastes, and using every possible artifice to inveigle him into buying and bargaining. He felt that everything that was taking place around him was a game, which he either knew, or thought he knew, because he grasped its meaning immediately—a childish, passionately eager game full of cunning and art, a game of looking into each other's hearts and guessing what was inside them, a game full of excitement, anger and bright good cheer, eternally alluring and gloriously entertaining.

He watched the craftsmen squatting before their open shops. They sat either in their doorways or on the pavement, surrounded by their wares, talking, shouting, laughing and chastising or fondling their children. Whenever the refrain of a song was wafted toward them, they would join in, as though, being lovers of order, they must perforce mend and patch up the snatches of melody torn from the general uproar, or felt it incumbent upon them to use the conductor's baton. But this did not prevent them from working both fast and skillfully. Lucas smiled back when they smiled up at him, and answered them when they addressed him eagerly as though they were picking up the threads of a conversation that had just been interrupted.

At one shop-door he caught sight of a gleaming array of figures. Closely packed, one above another, were numbers of small statues, goblets, dishes, busts, miniature columns, and all kinds of splendid vessels, in dazzling white plaster, shining tin, dark gold bronze, or ruddy copper. There were also a few pieces in veined marble that looked quite lifelike. Shining through the darkness of the shop and standing outlined in the twilight of the room, a dim, eloquent array of forms and figures, they loomed through the narrow opening of the door like riches bursting out of a cornucopia and falling at Lucas's feet. He halted, filled with such surprise and delight that at first his eyes could only stray in helpless bewilderment over the mass of forms, heads and ornaments. It took some time before he could really see and distinguish individual objects.

There stood a graceful Pallas, not more than seventeen inches high, but the majestic pose of the figure had an impelling grace that charmed him. Close by, on a copper basin, a beautifully chased lion's head thrust its muzzle toward him. Further on a slender silver goblet rose to view, flaunting its luxurious arms and bearing its molded cover like a crown. Figures of women stood delicately sinuous, with arms gracefully uplifted supporting a marble shell. There was also a bronze Perseus, holding the Gorgon's head in his outstretched hand.

Lucas was lost in admiration as he examined it. He noticed how an expression of faint physical revulsion and one of triumphant pride struggled for mastery in the noble, boyish features of the Perseus. Lucas trembled with delight to think that such marvels of art existed, that at last he was in the country where they were created, and that he could understand them with the consummate ease with which a man understands his mother tongue. So that was Perseus! And that was the right way to fashion him, with that conflict of feeling expressed in his face that made him seem so real! Lucas felt that an important secret had been revealed to him.

Some force, of which he suddenly became conscious, compelled him to turn away from the Perseus. In the narrow doorway stood a man, looking intently at him. He was a young fellow with curly black hair, and before him on a high turn-table stood a little gray figure in clay, on which he was working. Questioningly Lucas and the young man gazed into each other's eyes as though they had known each other for years.

The young man was the first to smile. "A fine piece!" he observed courteously, indicating the Perseus by a nod of the head.

"Did you do it?" whispered Lucas in awed tones.

The young man laughed. "I do it? How could I do anything like that? It comes from Florence. Do you know Florence?"

Lucas blushed. "No . . . but I am on my way there."

"Where from?"

"From Vienna."

The young man scanned his features intently.

"Vienna. That's a long way." Lured as by a spell, Lucas had unconsciously drawn closer to the little clay figure on the turn-table.

"I was in Florence for three years," observed the young man. "I was taught there."

"What is your name?" interrupted Lucas. "My name is Lucas Grassi. What is yours?"

"Agostino Cassana."

"How splendid that I should have met you!" cried Lucas, "and that you should have studied in Florence. I am going there for the same purpose as you did, you see. I want to learn. My father was an artist before me; he came from Tuscany and went to Vienna because they are building Palaces there. But I was only a child then. And now I want to go to Florence."

"Go to Cesare Bandini," said Agostino with a smile. "You won't find a better master in all Italy."

"Was he yours?"

Agostino nodded. "Just tell him you come from me. He was very fond of me; he did not want to let me go."

"Why didn't you stay with him?"

"I am a native of Verona. Besides, why should I have stayed there? I had been there three years! It isn't as if I could have become a Cesare Bandini. Agostino Cassana I am, and Agostino Cassana I must remain!"

They both laughed heartily.

Presently Agostino asked Lucas how long he had been in Verona.

The recollection of the previous day, when he had run about Verona as a dog, flashed through his mind. "I arrived here only this morning—before dawn," he replied.

"Have you seen the Can Grande yet?"

Lucas had never even heard of the Can Grande.

Throwing down his modelling tools, Agostino swathed the little figure in wet cloths and wiped his hands on his smock. "Come along!" he cried, as though in a great hurry.

They elbowed their way together through the surging crowd on the market-place, hearing and seeing nothing about them, so absorbed were they in their own conversation. They did not even notice that they had to shout to make themselves heard.

Lucas was describing all the dreams and desires he had cherished in solitude. He was aching to build, to carve statues, to paint pictures, and to chase vessels of gold and silver. Agostino laughed encouragingly as he confided all his plans to him, and was full of understanding and delight. It was all perfectly possible and must certainly be accomplished, and it could be accomplished by force of will. Why not? Agostino discussed the hewn stone and columns of the Palaces, the secret of their proportions, their color, the smoothness of the distempered walls, the durability of stretched canvas, of marble and gold, and all the tricks of the trade that happened to occur to him, as well as the peculiarities of the materials used, which were learned only by years of work on them. But as far as he himself was concerned, his one ambition was to be a sculptor. He wanted to carve statues of saints for the churches, and silver groups for the tables of grand nobles. He had commissions, and fresh orders came in every day. He was beginning to be well known. The little shop was not the only place he worked in. Later on, he said, he would have a large workshop with assistants and pupils.

Going down a narrow passage, they came to a standstill on a little square in front of a small church. On the side wall there was a sarcophagus of a man, flanked by pillars supporting a tall tapering roof, on the top of which stood an equestrian statue outlined against the blue of the sky.

Agostino pointed up. "The Can Grande," he said, and gazed expectantly at Lucas.

Above their heads the stone rider on the draped horse kept vigil. The tourney-helmet hanging over his back made him look as though he had wings, the sword in his hand was pointing upward, straight and solemn, ready for any emergency.

"Very old," whispered Agostino.

Lucas gazed up in silent reverence. The statue,

soaring above the shadow of the wall, bathed in sun-light, with the cool spring breeze playing about it, set Lucas aflame with enthusiasm. The sudden violent emotion threw wide the portals of his soul, drew it up to the heights, and flung it far away from its former plane into infinity.

"It is small," said Agostino, "but one does not notice that. As one goes away one remembers it as a big thing, a fine monument."

But Lucas did not hear what he was saying.

"Wandering about the animated streets, they talked and laughed as though they had known each other all their lives.

"How long are you staying in Verona?" Agostino enquired, as they took leave of one another.

"I don't know," stammered Lucas, turning pale.

"Which way do you want to go?" asked Agostino. "Did you come through Vicenza?"

Lucas did not reply.

Agostino became pressing. "You must go through Vicenza," he exclaimed, in tones of entreaty. "It is a little bit out of your way from here, but not much. Take my advice and go through Vicenza, and just have a look at the Rotunda there—you know the one I mean?—by Palladio . . . and then go to Padua. Donatello's wooden horse is there . . . then on to Ferrara. . . ."

Lucas knew that he would have to be a dog on the journey across country toward his goal. He knew that it would not depend upon himself how long he remained in Verona, nor would he be able to choose the road. And he was overcome with shame and fear.

"Come to me tomorrow," Agostino continued eagerly. "Then I shall be able to tell you exactly how to plan your journey. . . ."

"All right . . . tomorrow . . ." replied Lucas.

The Archduke entered Bologna in grand state.

As the procession drove along the sunlit road toward the walls of the city, the chimes of a hundred bells rang out to greet them. Cannon were fired from the ramparts, short sharp bursts of thunder breaking the stillness of the spring morning, while the cheers from the vast crowd above their heads were wafted down to them like the rustling of tall trees.

The Archduke alighted from his coach and went forward to meet the bright little group awaiting him at the city gates. There was the Cardinal, his scarlet robes conspicuous against the more somber garb of the figures about him. Surrounded by his priests, knights and councillors, he waited until the Archduke came up, receiving the Prince's kiss on his hand with regal majesty, after which he bowed respectfully to his guest. He was a handsome young man, tall, narrow-shouldered, and his face pale with the warm, mellow pallor of ivory. His eyes, like his hair and arched brows, were a deep, shining black, while his careless, genial manner was as attractive as it was dignified and balanced. The Archduke, who felt bashful in his presence, quickly turned to the others, and for a while the little group outside the walls laughed and chatted together. The bells were still ringing and the people cheering, as the cannon continued to boom above their heads.

When at last the procession trotted through the gates

amid the ring of horses' hooves, the clank of arms and the rattle of wheels, the din and clatter were unspeakable. The streets inside the town now lay open to view, lined with curious townsfolk, waving handkerchiefs and caps and cheering lustily. Slowly the procession advanced; the Archduke and the Cardinal, sitting side by side with nothing to say to each other, bowed right and left.

"What a beautiful dog you have," observed the Cardinal, as they alighted from the coach at the Palace. "What is his name?"

"Cambyses."

"I see, I see—the great names of the ancient world," observed the Cardinal, smiling. "Nowadays we have no other use for them so we call our dogs by the names of heathen kings and deities. . . ."

The Archduke was at a loss for a reply.

"What say you," the Cardinal continued, and there was a tinge of mockery in his voice, "do you think that one day our world will have sunk so low that people will call their dogs after our great kings and popes?" He saw that the Archduke looked puzzled, and apparently anxious to put him at his ease, he stopped short. "Just look at your dog," he added presently, "how devoutly he is looking up at the statue of Pope Julius. Isn't it strange? He saw the statue high up above the gate even before I could point it out to you myself. He looks as though he might even be admiring it."

The Archduke glanced up from his dog to the great statue, which throned it above the gate in solemn majesty.

"Who can tell what he sees up there?" he replied.

"You are right," said the Cardinal, smiling again. "Who knows why an animal like that looks up at the sky, and who can tell what he sees up there? But at all events he does not see a magnificent work of art—showing that after all he has something in common with certain bipeds!"

And with a haughty shrug of his shoulders, he entered the Palace with the Archduke.

As soon as he was himself again, Lucas roamed about the streets of Bologna. Standing in front of the Palace, he contemplated the statue of Julius II, reveling in the way this great and masterful monument lent gravity, character and eloquence to the facade with which it was so boldly blended. He examined the facade of the Palace, delighted with the wealth of mysterious science that was daily being revealed to him, and the number of artistic secrets that had been unveiled before his eyes since he had been in this country. He stood before the Palaces of the Bentivoglio and the Maffei; he visited the churches when they were empty, and paid his tributes of devotion to the altar-pieces, the statues and the carvings. This country offered him all those things for which his soul had been starving; it surrounded him with an atmosphere so familiar and awakened so many hidden instincts that he was constantly stirred to the depths. It was only with the utmost difficulty that he succeeded in suppressing a word that was continually rising to his lips: Home. No, he must not pronounce that word yet! He was still a long way from his goal. For the time being he was nothing but a miserable dog. His master could kill him if he chose; any low brute of a stable-boy could beat him to death. He might lie by the roadside, or perish in the gutter, before they reached Florence. No, that word must not pass his lips until they had arrived, until the terrible fate that held him in its toils had been fulfilled, and left him a free man once more.

One evening, as he was making his way with the crowd along the narrow street in front of the leaning Torre Asinelli, his foot struck against a small object which gave a faint ring. Bending over he picked up a purse, the worn leather folds of which he quickly unfastened. It contained only a few silver pieces and one gold coin, but to him it was the fulfilment of his heart's desire. Until that day he had been a beggar on the roads, wandering through strange cities and along unfamiliar paths, unable to buy so much as a crust of bread. He had eaten his fill only when the dog Cambyses had been fed, and had found somewhere to lay his head only when Cambyses was allowed to occupy a place in the straw. But now his fingers clutched the key to a little manly freedom. The anxiety that had so long oppressed him with regard to what he would do to earn a livelihood when he reached Florence, fell like a load from his heart.

Full of joy, he now took up his stand before the Palace, watching the constant animation and bustle at its gates. And every other day he became part of that bustle. He was a member of the throng within its gates, familiar with every corner of the stables, the stairs, the corridors, rooms, apartments and halls of the building. The day following he would stand outside it, apparently completely isolated, invisible and free. Hitherto, on his human days, filled with qualms that made him tremble, and a sense of shame that depressed him strangely, he had always avoided the proximity of the Archduke's train. On this particular day, however, he took up his stand before the Palace gates, overcoming both his qualms and his sense of shame, which constantly threatened to get the upper hand, and watched the familiar figures of the grooms, Count Waltersburg, fat Master Pointner and the others. All unsuspecting, they passed close by him. He knew all about them, every line in their faces, every movement of their shoulders, every detail of their ways was known to him, their voices, their desires, and the kindness and hardness of their hearts. But, suspecting nothing, they scarcely vouchsafed him a glance; had they gazed into his eyes for hours, still they would have suspected nothing. They knew only Cambyses, the dog; of Lucas, the man, they knew nothing.

The one person with whom he did not come face to face on these days was the Archduke himself, catching only a fleeting glimpse of him one morning in his coach, as he had done in Vienna on that first dismal November day. As he leaned back in the cushions the Archduke's thin face wore a haughty, disdainful expression and his blue eyes swept the rows of spectators with an expression of contemptuous indifference. But Lucas was anxious to see him at close quarters, as he had seen Count Waltersburg and Pointner, the Groom-of-the-Chamber. Without quite knowing why, he felt impeled to do this. An irresistible impulse, prompted neither by affection nor hostility, urged him to meet the Archduke face to face if he possibly could.

And he succeeded. One quiet afternoon he chanced

to enter the church of San Petronio, and was wandering, a lonely figure, from altar to altar, and statue to statue, when suddenly the Archduke, accompanied by the Cardinal and a magnificent retinue of courtiers, entered the silent precincts. They were all talking loudly and the lofty vaulted arches echoed their voices. Lucas crept behind a column.

"It was here that your Grace's great ancestor, Charles V, was crowned," Lucas heard the Cardinal say as the group came to a standstill close beside him.

The Archduke took a short step forward, and was about to reply when he found himself face to face with Lucas. He drew back, turned his head in confusion, coughed, tried to pull himself together; but Lucas gazed at him with a calm, curious, almost imploring look. Everything he had thought and experienced during the last few weeks unconsciously shone out of his eyes, as he stood for the first time erect in human form before his master; and for a few seconds he held the Archduke's eyes beneath the spell of his own, allowing him no escape.

Embarrassed and indignant at his own discomfiture, the Archduke raised his hand.

"What does that ragged lout over there want?" he whispered, turning to the Cardinal.

At a sign from the latter, two gentlemen went up to Lucas, motioning him to go and threatening and upbraiding him.

"Get out!" they hissed. "Be off at once!"

Slowly Lucas left the church.

The Archduke was breathing heavily. He thrust out his lower lip.

"How rudely the fellow stared!"

"Yes, he certainly had strange eyes," was the Cardinal's calm rejoinder.

"So you noticed them too?" observed the Archduke, shaking his head thoughtfully. "Those eyes . . . I can't think what they reminded me of. . . ."

On the following evening it happened that a farewell banquet was being given in honor of the Archduke, who was leaving for Florence the next day. It was a merry crowd that assembled round the board, eating and drinking their fill of the good fare spread before them. The dog tried to find a place to lie down, squeezing between the chairs and sitting down in front of the sideboard. But he could not find a suitable spot. At last he stretched himself on the floor at the far end of the table where the young Italian noblemen were seated.

Presently one of the latter rose and tried to get behind the other chairs to toast a friend who was sitting close to the Archduke. He was already slightly the worse for drink, and stumbled over the dog, who sprang to his feet in terror and tried quickly to get out of the way. But as he moved the young nobleman gave him such a vicious kick that the wretched animal, howling with pain, collapsed on the floor. Whereupon the young man set about venting his fury on the dog in good earnest.

"Just you wait, you confounded brute," he roared, "I'll teach you to trip me up!"

The dog's howl of pain and distress suddenly changed to a fierce growl of rage. Still smarting from the kick, he sprang furiously at the man, and with his forepaws on his shoulders, with one bound forced him against the wall. In a trice, the hubbub in the banqueting hall was silenced. Two or three of the revellers had jumped to their feet, and the only sound that broke the stillness was the low savage growl of the dog and the angry groan of the astonished and terrified man who, with the dog's jaws at his throat, was standing, white as death, with his back to the wall as though he were being crucified.

The dog was barking loudly in his victim's face. It sounded like a howl of hatred and reproach, and Pointner, behind his master's chair, quickly whispered to him what had happened. The young nobleman had just succeeded in drawing his dagger from its sheath when the Archduke brought his fist down heavily on the table.

"You dare touch a hair of my dog's coat!" he roared. "How dare you kick my dog, you drunken sot! Put up your dagger, I say!"

Immediately the dog released his enemy, dropped on all fours, and stood perfectly still. The tongue hanging out of his mouth alone betrayed his state of exhaustion. He was still growling with indignation.

The young nobleman, ashamed and sobered, his clothes all disarranged, came away from the wall.

"Pon my soul, Messer Giovanni," came the Cardinal's calm voice, addressing him from the other end of the room, "you are certainly drunk, and you are an ill-mannered lout! Leave the hall at once, sir!"

Messer Giovanni crept noiselessly from the hall and the dog followed him as far as the door.

The dark woodland through which they had been laboriously climbing hour after hour had depressed the Archduke's spirits. But, sitting inside the slowly advancing coach he had suddenly become aware that the road was growing flat again, that it was beginning to grow lighter, that a vast expanse of bright blue sky was gradually becoming visible, and that the screen of boughs and twigs through which the sun was shining was steadily growing thinner. And as the cavalcade suddenly emerged from the trees into open fields, he began to breathe more freely. Suddenly he leaned out and called a halt.

The cuirassiers, eager to follow the gently sloping road into the valley, had already started off at a trot, but drawing rein, they turned the horses on to the grass by the side of the road and leaped down from their saddles. The column scattered right and left, and the rest of the carriages, with the pack-mules and the Archduke's baggage-wagons, which had yet to come up, began to pour higgledy-piggledy out of the woods.

The fields stretched in radiant softness down the slope toward the valley. In a moment a throng of gaily dressed folk had spread over them. The sound of voices filled the air, to the accompaniment of the clank of chains and arms, the rattle of wheels, the creaking of saddles and harness, the stamping and neighing of horses, and the hubbub set up by the servants, busily taking hampers from the wagons in order to prepare a meal and arrange for the comfort of the company.

A little way off the Archduke was walking up and down a piece of open ground with Count Waltersburg. He seemed in good spirits. Pointner followed them while the dog frolicked about.

Far below in the distance, glowing in the rays of the sun, Tuscany beckoned invitingly to them. Its bright green fields extended as far as eye could see to the shimmering sapphire of the hills beyond, while dotted far and wide over the carpet of turf the white marble houses of town and village flashed their light up to the heights, and cupolas and turrets shone like precious stones.

"Is that Florence over there?" asked the Archduke, pointing.

Count Waltersburg peered into the distance with the air of an expert. "'Pon my soul, I do not know," he replied at last.

Pointner began to laugh, and Waltersburg turned round in a huff.

"Just look, Your Grace, how that dog is standing!" cried Pointner. "He looks exactly as though he too were wondering whether it is Florence or not. . . ."

They all turned to look at the dog who was standing with his neck stretched out and his ears pricked, looking down into the valley.

"Well, Cambyses," said the Archduke, smiling and

bending down to pat him, "perhaps you know whether that is Florence?"

The dog cringed with fear at his touch, but quickly raised his head to his master, ran forward a few steps, and then stopped still again, as though to examine the landscape once more.

They took no further notice of him.

Presently when the Archduke had sat down to table with Count Waltersburg, Pointner, who was waiting on them, suddenly exclaimed: "Whom is Cambyses making such a fuss about over there?"

Turning they saw an old man with a gray beard emerging from the undergrowth, bowing to all sides, and talking, laughing and calling the dog, who was gamboling round him in a mad dance of joy, yelping with delight.

The Archduke frowned and sprang to his feet. "Strange," he murmured, and obviously put out, advanced toward the couple. The others followed.

Neither the old man nor the dog noticed their approach. The dog seemed to be completely beside himself, and ran breathless round and round the man, now jumping violently up at him, as though he wanted to knock him down or embrace him, now scampering away as though daring the man to catch him. The man bent round and twisted about, until his little knapsack slid from his back up his neck, and laughed in bewildered delight.

"Yes, well, what do you want?" he repeated softly. "What's the matter with you? . . . Yes . . . Good dog! . . . Are we such friends then, for you to make such a fuss over me? . . . Yes. . . . Ha! . . . I never did. . . . Have you gone mad? . . . Yes, good dog! . . . But I tell you I don't know you. . . ."

"I say, you fellow!"

At the sudden sound of the Archduke's voice the old man started with fear, and his flustered movement forced the former, who had come close up to him, to step back a pace or two. The old man gazed in astonishment at the young Prince and his companions.

"A crazy dog!" he exclaimed with a smile. But the stern expression in the Archduke's eyes covered him with confusion. "A . . . crazy . . . dog!" he stammered under his breath.

"What's all this about the dog? What do you want with him?" demanded the Archduke with cold severity.

But the old man had already regained his self-possession and was laughing quite innocently.

"Well that's funny. What do I want with him? What I would like to know is what the dog wants with me? Don't you see? God in heaven!" he exclaimed turning round angrily to Pointner, who had knocked his hat off his head. And looking furiously from one to the other, he was on the point of flinging himself without further ado on the Groom-of-the-Chamber. "I say, look here, you! . . ."

"You must not keep your hat on in the presence of His Imperial Highness," said Pointner calmly, seizing his wrist.

The old man gave a little start of surprise. His arm dropped limply to his side, and calming down, he subjected the Archduke to a silent though kindly scrutiny. Then he gave a short whistle.

"Oh indeed!" he drawled. He looked at the dog,

who was standing watching and wagging his tail. "Oh indeed!" he repeated about half an octave higher as if he were just beginning to understand.

"Who are you?" demanded the Archduke.

"Oh, it's easy enough to see what the fellow is," Count Waltersburg interposed haughtily. "A tramp! Take a whip, Pointner, and drive the ragamuffin away."

"Now, now," exclaimed the old man, drawing himself up. He stood proudly and stiffly before them, his vivacious little eyes sparkling, and his second "Now!" ringing out loud and defiant. "I am not a tramp! I cannot allow that!"

"What the devil . . . !" ejaculated Waltersburg.

But the old man shouted him down.

"Nothing to do with the devil, my Lord Count Waltersburg. . . . Yes, don't you see? Yes, his lordship may well stare! But I have seen you often enough, when you were only so high . . . yes, indeed . . . with your noble father . . . of course . . . and I won't stand being thrashed!" He laughed again and glanced from one to the other with his merry flashing eyes.

"Who are you?" the Archduke enquired in low, contemptuous tones.

The old man gave him a friendly nod as though he quite agreed with him. "That's how it is," he said, wagging his head. "His Imperial Highness has already asked me that question, and if my Lord Count will allow me to reply, I will give you all the information you require. . . ." And he winked merrily at the Count.

"Quick!" commanded the Archduke.

"At your service!" replied the old man with unruffled serenity. "I am Master-Tailor Wendelin Knapps of Prague. . . ." And he laughed. "Yes, indeed, of Prague, my Lord Count. And your noble father often used to come to my shop, and bring you with him; but in those days you were only a little chap."

"Then what are you doing here, out all alone in the wide, wide world?" exclaimed Count Waltersburg in surprise.

The old man proceeded to explain, as though what he was saying were all a matter of course. "Well, just having a look round . . . taking a look at the wide, wide world . . . strolling about in fact. I heard of a country where it was always spring, and tales of the sea . . ." he was almost chanting now, "the sea. . . ."

"What do you want with that dog?" the Archduke repeated impatiently.

"Yes, of course . . . the dog. . . ." The old man hesitated. His face became a blank. "I don't know the dog," he answered at last.

The Archduke, conscious of the opposition in the old man's attitude, became embarrassed. "You lie . . ." he stammered.

Shrugging his shoulders, the old man turned away. "Well, for all I care, it may be a lie," he muttered softly to himself.

Pointner, noticing the embarrassment in his master's face, came up to him. "It is quite possible the old man is speaking the truth," he said. "In fact, I feel pretty certain he is. How could the fellow possibly know Cambyses? Dogs like this often have crazy whims. . . . Some peculiar smell about a man, or something of the sort, is quite enough . . . isn't that so? We humans may notice nothing, but a fellow comes along with something peculiar about him and the dogs go straight up to him and lick his hands. And another time they'll bark at a man, and be nearer tearing him to bits than playing with him. How can we tell what goes on in a dog's mind?"

The Archduke had resumed his cold and haughty expression. "How can we tell what goes on in a dog's mind?" he repeated slowly, and looked across at Cambyses lying on the ground, intently watching every one of the old man's movements, and beating the grass madly with his tail.

"I'll have the brute shot!" he said sternly, turning round and going back to his place. "Either today or tomorrow."

Pointner followed him. "Oh, Your Imperial Highness, pray don't do that!" he begged. "That would be a great pity! Perhaps you might give him away. After all, he does run away every other minute, and there's no holding him. A strange brute, but such a beautiful dog! Shoot him? . . . Surely there's no need for that! It would be such a pity! It would be no use—such a fine beast too!"

The Archduke did not seem to be listening.

The old man pretended to be busy with his knap-sack, but he kept a sharp eye on all that was taking place around him, and when the gentlemen had sat down to table again, he strolled carelessly on step by step along the edge of the wood, skirted a coppice that abutted into the field, and, concealed from the Archduke's party, descended the grassy slope.

The dog came creeping up behind him, with a short, low, impatient whine.

"I know . . . yes, I know . . ." said the old man in kind soothing tones. "I know. . . . I know all about it. Even if you could speak, I could not understand you better. Yes, yes . . . just be quiet . . . I understand all about you . . . I understand everything."

The dog lashed his hindquarters with his tail, yawned impatiently, sighed and gazed into the old man's face.

They were both silent for a moment. Presently the old man laughed light-heartedly. "Nice of you, old dog-gie, to have been so pleased to see me," he said. "Nice of you that was! I am pleased to see you too...." Then with a jerk of his head to the rear, he added: "They would have given their ears to know what was up between us two." And he laughed merrily again, his little eyes sparkling. "But what do they know about friends like us—eh?"

The dog sat quite still, with his ears pricked up.

"Down there lies your beloved Florence," he went on almost reverently, stretching out his hand and pointing to the glowing plain below.

The dog made a short sharp sound like a sob.

"But . . . let it be!" And the old man made a quick defensive movement with his arm. "Let it be! You can do nothing to make things different now. . . . It would be no use at all." He shook his head and added softly. "I don't know how this happened to you . . . and you say you don't know either. Well then. . . . But I fancy things won't be very different for you from what they are for anybody else who has nothing in the world. Who knows what you may have wished for yourself . . . who knows how you wished yourself into your present

plight. . . . Yes, that's probably how it came about. . . .
You did not dare to ask for too much . . . eh? Yes, yes . . .
people like us always imagine one has to pay forevery
bit of luck . . . and so we always pay much more than we
need . . . no courage . . . no daring . . . one is only a poor
wretch of a dog, you see!"

And so the old man went on in low animated tones,
as though he were replying to all kinds of objections.

"But how's that then? . . . How is one to make one's
way . . . ? Absurd. One isn't even asked, one is simply given one's lot. . . . That's how it is. One man gets
everything, another nothing at all, and everyone has to
make the best of things as long as he is on earth. Ha! it
would be much better if everybody were asked what
they would like their lot on earth to be . . . that would
be much better! But then the muddle on earth would
be even greater than it is already. . . . No need to argue
about that. . . . One can see with one's own eyes how
matters stand when a man is allowed to have his wish
in such matters. It is always the same. . . . Mark my
words . . . always the same! And then a poor devil of a

man complains that he has such a wretched lot, such a miserably wretched lot. . . ."

The old man heaved a comic sigh. "Oh God, oh God!" he exclaimed, with a low laugh. "Well, and then a fairy comes along, a perfidious fairy, or some other artful dodger of a spirit . . . how can one describe such a creature? . . . And it says the poor devil of a man can have a wish . . . three wishes . . . !" He whistled merrily. "And lo and behold! the poor devil wishes himself something . . . and then he is a much poorer devil than he was before. . . .

"I know all about it," he continued, growing serious. "And I always say this wishing business is no damned good! If a man is poor, wishing won't make him rich and if he's unhappy, wishing won't make him happy!"

They were sitting close up to each other looking out over the sun-bathed landscape at their feet.

The next day Lucas woke up to find himself on the road to Florence. He danced for joy and when he felt tired and thought he would sit down to rest, he found it quite impossible to keep still. So the only rest he took was to slacken his pace, comforting himself with the reflection that even the slowest crawl took him forward. When he came to cross-roads, he would point straight in front of him and call out to passers-by: "To Florence?" And they would either nod, or show him the proper way. And every answer they vouchsafed him he regarded as a gift, an occasion for rejoicing, for it confirmed him in his belief that he was nearing his goal. As the day slipped by he became exhausted. Hunger gnawed at his entrails like a demon; his mouth and throat were scorched with thirst, and he was covered from head to foot with the fine white dust of Tuscany.

It occurred to him that his impatient forced march was not in the least necessary; for could he not cover the distance quite comfortably in the Archduke's coach, and meanwhile stroll about at his leisure in the glorious country? After all, when the hour struck his Fate would snatch him away to Florence willy nilly. But the very idea made him shudder with horror. It was precisely that possibility that he wished at all costs to escape. He must enter Florence as a man! He must be himself on

that great day! That had been his one prayer throughout the long and tedious journey. On no account must
he enter the land of promise a damned and degraded
creature. And the fear with which the thought inspired
him whipped on his flagging footsteps.

From the vine-clad hills of Pistoia he looked down
on Florence lying at his feet. The glory of her marble
Palaces, her towers, cupolas and spires, blended by the
mist in lavish confusion and luxuriant clusters like some
exotic tropical creeper, reminded him of a loud chorus
of voices filling the air with the strains of a hymen of
praise. The sight infused fresh energy into him. But the
day was slowly waning, the road sloped gently step by
step down into the plain, and the inspiring magnetic
picture of the city beckoning to him became shrouded
in the veil of twilight.

Night had fallen, and it was already dark before
he stood at last before the city gates. "I have to get to
Cesare Bandini," he said boldly, when the watchman
challenged him, and his heart stopped beating at the
thought that he might be forbidden to enter.

"Are you a pupil of Maestro Bandini?" the official inquired in kindly tones.

Lucas laughed with relief. "Certainly I am his pupil. Please let me pass, I must go to him."

"This very night? So late?"

"It is not as late as all that, either for the Maestro or for me," he pleaded, but stopped short, overcome by qualms.

"Bandini is waiting," he added hurriedly. "I have important news for him." It was a lie, but it served its purpose.

"Well then, run along," said the watchman, slapping him on the shoulder. And Lucas ran.

Hurrying through a couple of dark narrow courts, he suddenly stopped short, and leaning wearily against a wall, burst into tears. His arms hung limp at his sides; his face was turned slightly upward, so that he might have seen the stars shining in the little streak of sky between the roofs of the houses. But he saw nothing. He sobbed silently to himself, until his heart beat less fiercely and his breathing grew easier. He brushed the

tears away, heaved a little sigh, and continued on his journey. Suddenly he felt comforted. A fierce uncontrollable
joy blazed slowly up in his breast and the reverent hope
that filled it robbed the weariness from his limbs.

At first he marveled to see the people he passed
going about so calmly, as though it were the most ordi-
nary thing in the world to be in Florence. Undecided
whither to turn, he stopped at every street corner and
looked round. His heart was bursting with longing to see
the city, even at that late hour—to see it all, the cathedral,
Brunelleschi's Baptistry, the Campanile, and above all
Michelangelo's David. His father had always spoken with
reverence of this statue of David; Agostino Cassana, the
young sculptor of Verona, had referred to it in hushed
and solemn tones, and Lucas had dreamed of it on his
way. His agitated heart rose up in rebellion against the
mantle of darkness which hid the city from his gaze, as
if it were grudging him a glimpse of its glories.

Nevertheless he continued on his way, impatient
yet confident, obstinately determined to feast his eyes
on as much as the darkness would allow. Suddenly the

narrow alley he had been ascending broadened and he found himself in a wide open space, where the Arno flowed past like a dim shimmering belt of silver before his eyes, and he could hear the gentle murmur of its waters. Lights were twinkling in the windows of many of the houses, and at no very great distance away he could see lights and torches in the street. He made his way toward them, thinking that at last he had discovered the heart of the city. Suddenly he stopped.

Straight across the river he thought he saw a cloud hanging very low.

Then as he drew nearer he gradually became aware that it was not a cloud. Stranger far, a gray mass of stone consisting of small houses stood suspended over the river—a bridge the like of which he had never seen before. It might have been one of the narrow old courts or alleys lifted bodily and laid across the river to serve as a bridge. And he felt more indignant than ever that the night had dropped a veil before his eyes, to mar his first sight of the city.

But as the marvellous stone structure loomed mistily

before his eyes, his excitement grew tenser, as little by little he knew how many of his wishes were already being fulfilled.

He turned it all over in his mind. Everything that he had yearned for—nay, more than he had ever hoped for in his wildest dreams, already compassed him about. It was all there, together with a hundred and one surprises that lay hidden from view. He seemed to be surrounded by gifts. Enveloped in a veil of darkness though they were, their lavish profusion could nevertheless be divined; as a child on the eve of its birthday is allowed to take a swift glance at what awaits him, without entirely removing the wrapper from his presents, so Lucas now resolved to savor the sweets of expectation for yet a while longer.

The sound of singing close by made him turn round, and he ran along the bank in the direction from which it came. He soon found himself in the middle of a crowd which grew thicker and thicker as he advanced. He peered into their faces, and examined their costumes, which were now quite bright and clear and the next moment dim and indistinct, as the light from the torches and the swinging lamps fell upon them or buried them in shadow.

Exulting, he slipped in among the crowd as it merrily sauntered along, singing and shouting, and was borne away from the riverbank into the maze of narrow streets close by which echoed the festive clamor. He saw that he was approaching nearer and nearer the heart of the city. It mattered not to him where he went, for the hour of his transformation was close at hand, and whatever happened he would be provided with a bed and shelter for the remainder of the night.

Suddenly one wish alone possessed his heart—to reach the Palace in front of which Michelangelo's David kept watch and ward. Even if it were only in semi-darkness, or beneath the fitful flare of the torches, he longed to stand before the white marble statue, to pay his respects to it for the first time that day, while he was still himself.

It occurred to him that he might ask one of the crowd about him. But an extraordinary feeling of shyness prevented him from doing so, and a playful spirit of curiosity prompted him to see whether he could not hit upon the way himself. He saw squares spreading out before him, the sound of music broke on his ear, magnificent doors, crowned and framed by stone figures, turned their proud inscrutable faces toward him. In the middle of one square, a church soared aloft to heaven. The Duomo! Lucas muttered to himself; but he did not slacken his pace, and with a sudden superhuman effort of self-control, did not allow his eyes even to glance up to try to discern the outline of the edifice through the darkness.

Jostled right and left, he would unexpectedly find himself isolated, and would hurry back to the crowd, until at last he entered the largest square he had hitherto seen. Even then he did not guess how near he was to his goal, until suddenly, above the sea of heads about him, he caught sight of a shining white statue. He gasped for breath, and remained rooted to the spot, his feet refusing to carry him further. His heart beat wildly.

Further on, the Palace, with its tower and battlements,

reared its mighty walls into the darkness. At the corner the gate stretched its somber arch over the crowd, while just in front of it, as though he had just walked out, stood the David, his figure shining out white and luminous in the night. The details were not visible and his face was merely a white patch in the blackness.

Stiff as stone, Lucas stood gazing across the square. His heart whispered that he had now reached the end of his journey. The fact that he could not behold the David in all its beauty at that late hour suddenly struck him as being a merciful intervention on the part of Fate to spare him. For the moment, it seemed to him sufficient that he had succeeded in obtaining a glimpse of the statue; he had at least satisfied himself that day that it really existed.

For the first time in his life, his soul seemed to grasp the fact that this stone in human form was always there, day and night, year in, year out. The colossal indifference of the motionless marble figure stirred him to the depths. As if moved by a spell, he felt impeled to picture the day on which Michelangelo's warm and vital touch had rested on that stone for the last time, and the night that had followed that day—the first night, which had been as solitary and interminable as all the nights up to that moment. Suddenly he found himself unable to believe that Michelangelo had really lived and breathed, or that he was now dead and buried. It all seemed as strange and incredible as a fairy-tale.

And thus he stood for a long while gazing across at the shimmering whiteness of the statue.

The following morning Lucas was a dog again. Exhausted by his long tramp on the previous day and worn out by the excitement of his first stroll through the city, he lay curled up fast asleep. As the young stable-boy came in early in the morning, he almost fell over him.

"Quite right, he's back in his place again, is old Cambyses," he said with a laugh as he leaned over the dog, whose sides were rising and falling in heavy sleep.

And he set to work in the stables. The horses stamped and neighed, and other stable-boys arrived, laughing and singing and shouting to one another, and, calling to the horses at the tops of their voices, they began to groom their charges. But the dog lay there fast asleep, deaf to everything around him.

The young groom went up to him again and stood over him, shaking his head and calling the attention of the others to him.

"There's old Cambyses again. He's so fast asleep he might be a stone."

An old coachman held up a pail of water which he was carrying. "I'll show you how fast he can move," he said, coming up to the lad.

"No, for God's sake let him be!" cried the young groom, barring the way. "He's dead beat—dog tired!" he added with a laugh. "Who knows how long he's been tearing round, wearing himself to the bone!"

"He's a mad beast!" replied the old coachman. "Always racing off, the Lord alone knows where to, and always back again, God knows where from."

Across the white courtyard, now bathed in the bright light of the morning sun, Master Pointner was making his way toward the stable. The young groom immediately crouched down by the dog.

"Now then, wake up quick, Cambyses," he said, seizing him by the silky fur on his chest and shoulders and gently shaking him. "You mustn't sleep any longer now.... Pointner's coming.... He'll only kick you in the belly again.... Quick! Quick!"

The dog began to wag his tail, extending his slender, graceful legs in front of him so stiffly that they quivered, stretching his neck, and rubbing his head in the chaff on the ground. Meanwhile the groom had got up, and, running to the door, called out across the yard: "Master Pointner; Cambyses is back again!"

"Damn the brute!" cried Pointner irritably as he came up to the stall. "Miserable creature!" he growled, as he peered down at him in the straw.

In a flash the dog had sprung to his feet. His eyes moved strangely as though still seeing confused visions. His whole body quivered as though he were thrilled by the memory of some piece of good fortune, or had suddenly realised a dream. Enveloped in the pungent smell of horses, the scent of fresh sweet hay, and the penetrating fragrance of the gardens beyond, his heart and all his senses stimulated by the sun, the dog was for the moment well-nigh intoxicated.

"Miserable creature!" repeated Master Pointner. The dog replied with a short bark that sounded like an exclamation of joy, and began circling round him, in a series of wonderful high springs, as though he were trying to catch his own tail.

"Don't hurt him," pleaded the young groom, laughing. "Look how glad our old Cambyses is to be back again!"

"Glad!" shouted Master Pointner, "the rascal! See what the brute makes us put up with. . . ." He struck out at the dog, but the blow only cleaved the air.

"Damn the brute!" He struck out again and again, twisting and turning until he grew quite giddy. But all in vain. Suddenly, in a flash, the dog sprang at his chest. Light as a flock of down blown by the wind, he jumped, and before Master Pointner had time to wink an eyelid, he touched him gently with his paws, nudged him softly with his nose under the chin, and scampered out through the open door.

Staggering slightly, Pointner also dashed out into the courtyard, blustering and shouting orders. But the dog only gamboled the more wildly over the warm, dazzling white gravel, circling round Pointner at a respectful distance, and barking so lustily that he drowned every other sound. Pointner roared and raved; the two might almost have been carrying on an argument. The dog's bark sounded now like a note of jubilation, now like a cry of hatred, and yet again as though he were heaping reproaches on the head of the infuriated man. The young groom was holding his sides with laughter.

Everything seemed to be in festive mood. Spacious flowering gardens enclosed the bright courtyard on every side, the sky, a deep azure, shimmered in the flaming rays of the sun, while at the windows of the Palace heads could be seen popping in and out, calling, laughing and chattering. The broad marble steps, which were so shallow that to ascend them felt more like floating through air than climbing, were thronged with

gaily dressed people. The dog swept joyously up and
down the steps, now stopping and waiting for Pointner,
as though asking him "Whither?" then running back as
much as to say, "Faster please!" or "What are you waiting for?" Whereupon in a couple of mighty bounds he
would leap the stairs gracefully again. Seeing the crowds
about, Pointner suspended hostilities, and as the dog
sprang past, more than one hand was stretched out to
pat the lively creature.

He dashed gaily into the great hall, the door of
which Pointner had opened. It was a stately apartment;
huge, brightly colored pictures adorned its walls, while
through many a lofty window the sun poured in at a
sharp angle, gilding the floor with broad golden beams
of light. Here a throng of people stood solemnly congregated, and the dog, pushing his way unceremoni-
ously through them, was obliged to turn and look about
him to find his master. The latter, in a pale blue, gold-
embroidered uniform, was standing by a stately person-
age in purple velvet, surrounded by a circle of ladies.
Some of the company drew aside as the dog made his

way between them; there was a rustle of silk dresses and a little girl standing near the Archduke shrieked with fright. But as soon as the dog saw the child, he dropped to the floor and lay motionless.

"That's Cambyses, my traveling companion," said the Archduke with a laugh. "See, Elizabeth, he's quite tame."

The little girl began to smile timidly at the dog who still lay stretched on the ground, wagging his tail furiously. The whole company laughed.

"Well, Elizabeth," continued the Archduke, bending over the child and the dog, "shall we stroke him a little? He certainly does not deserve it, do you, Cambyses? He's constantly running away, or disappearing, and no one can find him anywhere. But he always comes back."

And he patted the dog's sides, while the little girl bent down timidly and stroked his back with the tips of her fingers. Cambyses kept quite still until the child had recovered from her fright. Then he got up gently, gazed long and intently at the pretty little fair-haired girl, and a moment later the two began to play together and were still doing so when the company went in to dinner. The guests had long ceased to pay any attention to them.

Throughout the banquet strains of music mingled with the clinking of vessels and the buzz of voices. At last the Grand Duke and His Imperial Highness rose from the table, followed by the rest of the company, and the day's festivities continued. The procession descended the stairs in regular order, like a bright-colored gleaming wave rolling downward in a shimmer of gold and sparkling jewels. In the courtyard state coaches were standing in readiness, and each one, as it slowly bowled away with its occupants, was escorted by a troop of magnificent bodyguards. As usual the dog ran by the side of the Archduke's carriage.

As they left the dark narrow streets, in which the clatter of the horses' hooves and the rattle of the wheels had been deafening, and suddenly emerged into a blaze of light, air and sunshine, amid gleaming white houses, the air was full of the murmur of voices. Crowds of people were massed beyond the trotting fence of bodyguards. A thousand waving arms formed a tangled lattice-work of limbs, while a thousand throats roared forth a torrent of cheers. It was like a living hedge, swayed hither and thither by a storm, laughing and roaring its greeting. Ever and anon the cheering would die down for a moment and a shrill, lonely voice be heard shouting alone, to be drowned immediately in the general tumult that quickly broke out afresh. The procession advanced slowly downhill, and on reaching the Arno, which gleamed like an emerald between its silvery banks, pressed on laboriously across the wonderful Ponte Vecchio and through the narrow alleys between the houses, until, on passing down a short street, it entered the square where stood the Town Hall with its tower, its battlements and traverses. Above the faces of the swarming crowd the marble head of the David gleamed white and majestic.

The Archduke's carriage pulled up immediately in front of the statue which marked the entrance to the Town Hall. The bodyguards who were keeping the crowd back and the gentlemen in gorgeous uniforms

who advanced toward the carriage to welcome the
Archduke had now neither the time nor the inclination
to take any notice of Cambyses. Had they been able to
watch him, they might have had cause to feel surprised
or possibly amused. The dog was struggling to raise his
eyes to the statue, though some invisible power was
drawing his nose to the ground. Twice, thrice he tried
to gaze up at the marble monument, but each time the
irresistible force exercised by all manner of scents drew
his nose down to the plinth. Obliged at last to yield to
the impulse, he sniffed quickly and uneasily round the
sides of the base, turned in anguish this way and that,
but could not tear himself away. At last, cocking his
leg up against the statue, he gazed in front of him with
bowed head and clouded eyes, full of dumb agony.

Lucas paused on the threshold of Bandini's house.

The artist's studios were on the ramparts close
to the city gates from which the road to Fiesole led
out. Lucas had had no difficulty in finding the place,
for everybody knew Cesare Bandini. As soon as he

pronounced the name a smile suffused the faces of those he questioned, and their eyes shone more brightly as they showed him the way. Thither he had gone in a spirit of the deepest reverence, lofty expectation and excitement which his joy and bashfulness made all the greater.

As he wandered through the city, hesitating and then hurrying on again, the very houses and Palaces seemed to be speaking to him, the statues, churches, gleaming marble towers and even the heavens addressed him, as did also the kindly sun and the people in the streets, cheerful, proud and graceful, guileless in their merry laughter and song. They all gave him the impression of being glad to be alive, glad to be at work; their very faces filled him with courage. His heart glowed every time he asked one of them the way to Cesare Bandini's house. The cheerful readiness with which they replied, the easy dignity of their bearing, the proud carriage of their heads, and the noble sincerity and courtesy of their smiling faces inspired him with a sense of power. And now as he stood at the entrance to Bandini's house, feeling both strong and brave, it seemed to him that he was on the threshold of a new and better life.

And lo! what was the first sight to catch his eye, but a group of three children on the grass, with arms uplifted holding a large shell above their heads. They were three boys between eight and ten years of age, with sturdy little brown bodies, on the pulsating flesh of which the verdant shadows of the trees kept up a constant play of light and shade. Ever and anon they would lower the shell; but only for a moment, and then they would raise it again in a slightly different pose, dancing, standing still, dancing again. A small gathering of young men were sitting on low stools on the grass round the lively group, drawing and modelling, or calling to the little boys and joking with them. One of them, catching sight of Lucas standing in the hall, sprang to his feet and hastened over to him.

"What is it you want?" he asked.

"I want to see Maestro Cesare Bandini," replied Lucas. He had uttered the words many times that morning but this time they had an anxious, resolute ring which implied that he refused to be turned away.

The young man smiled. He was a handsome youth with slender shoulders and thin, hollow cheeks; his pale brow rose in a noble curve to the black waves of hair, his eyes looked gentle and thoughtful, and the smile on his fresh lips was kindly. His smile was provoked by the anxious, defiant tone in Lucas's reply, and was intended to reassure him. He did not answer at once, and so Lucas began again. "I should like to. . . ."

"Important?" interrupted the young man. Lucas merely closed his eyes and raised his eyebrows.

"Over there!" The young man pointed to a long straggling shed, built along one side of the garden. It had several large windows looking out on to the lawn.

Lucas and his companion crossed the courtyard, passing through a medley of broken statues, busts, blocks of stone, heaps of scrap iron, old vases and paint pots. He would have liked to run but did not dare. They entered the garden where the naked children were now running about as they pleased. The other students only cast a fleeting glance at Lucas as he passed, and went on with their work. One or two of them were singing or whistling softly to themselves.

Lucas screwed up all his courage.

"Are you one of Bandini's pupils?" he enquired of his guide.

"I am Filippo Volta, the painter," the young man replied with a friendly smile.

By this time they had reached a glass door. "Just go in and keep quiet," said Filippo. "Don't attempt to say good-day or anything else. He doesn't like that sort of thing when he's at work. Just wait and say nothing. He'll speak to you all in good time."

Hardly daring to breathe, Lucas gave a silent nod. With a smile Filippo Volta left him and returned to his place.

Almost blind with excitement, Lucas entered. He stood still close to the door, gasping for breath and casting a quick nervous glance round the long white-washed room with its black rafters overhead. It took him some time to distinguish what was before him. Along the walls he saw picture after picture, framed and

unframed, depicting in luminous colors every aspect of
the human form. Female figures stood out in dazzling
beauty, posing majestically, with upraised arms, sinuous
hips, voluptuous shoulders, haughtily arched necks and
firmly rounded breasts. There too were men and youths
full of health and strength, in crested helmets and
gleaming golden armor; while landscapes with verdant
trees, rocky hills, green stretches of water, and deep blue
skies invited the eye. Between them, hanging by themselves in their frames, were the portraits of grave and
haughty nobles in their velvet court dresses with orders
on their breasts, queenly women resplendent in pearls
and brocade, gazing out on the spectator with expres-
sions stern or gentle. Lucas noticed that one of the walls
was hung with a woven Flemish tapestry representing
figures on a background of thick foliage, while scattered
between the screens and easels that stood about were
bronze statues, white marble busts, carved wooden figures painted in rich colors with gilt cloaks and crowns,
such as had recently begun to appear in the churches.
His eye also fell on wonderful cabinets, carved chairs

upholstered in Genoese velvet, helmets and armor.

As he stood silently at the door, Lucas's serenity and courage began to ebb. But he gradually recovered sufficient composure to examine the inmates of the room. He heard them talking to one another in short, broken sentences, without looking up from their work. But he was still too frightened to understand the sense of the words that fell in a confused jumble on his ear.

His attention was first attracted by a man close by him working at a turn-table. He was a short, bull-necked fellow with a ferocious expression, was modelling a group with wild infuriated movements of his hands. Nor far from him, seated in a luxurious armchair, was a man who appeared to be quite old, calmly working on a small picture. Lucas was surprised to see that he was wearing the tunic of an officer, with a captain's sash about his portly waist. His eager face was framed in a wealth of snow-white hair like flames of silver, while his bright red cheeks gave him an appearance of youthful exuberance. Beneath his large, aquiline nose was a thick white mustache; his full, voluptuous, red lips met in a pronounced pout. Lucas could see that the old man was working on a smooth, highly finished picture of a Madonna and that he was painting with calm but passionate absorption. His white mop of hair seemed to stand ever more and more on end with the efforts he was making, while his flushed brow burned like a furnace. He breathed loudly and heavily and from time to time would lean straight back, sit perfectly still, and give vent to a deep, almost inaudible groan. Occasionally, as he bent forward again to put another touch on the picture with his finely pointed brushes, he would sing under his breath in a pleasant, melodious voice; then he would stop and bury himself once more in his work, his breath coming short and fast like a swimmer struggling against the waves.

At last Lucas allowed his eyes to wander further into the room to catch a glimpse of Cesare Bandini. He knew at once that he was the Maestro. He was working at a picture which Lucas could not see, as it stood at too wide an angle. To see it, he would have had to step aside, and this he did not venture to do. Besides, for the moment it was sufficient to see Cesare Bandini before his very eyes. He stood there gazing at him, admiring him, already ardently drawn to him. He was painting without taking his eyes off his picture.

"Water!" cried the short, bull-necked man at the turn-table. It was the first word that Lucas not merely heard but also understood. A handsome little boy dashed forward, with fair, curly locks and cheeks as fat as a cherub's, dressed in a dirty smock bespattered with grease spots and blobs of paint. Creeping behind Cesare Bandini, he moved one or two paint-pots out of the way, removed a dripping sponge from the pail he carried and carefully moistened the clay.

"Is your Archduke a handsome fellow?" asked the short, bull-necked man meanwhile, addressing nobody in particular.

"I don't know," replied Bandini after a moment's silence, his voice ringing out like a bright melody.

"Is he coming soon?" growled the other.

"I don't know," chanted Bandini once more.

The thick-set man was working at his clay again

with the same ferocity as before. "Is he really coming here today?" he asked almost angrily.

Bandini went on painting. "Ye-es!" he replied in his deep sing-song voice.

"Ye-es!" echoed the fair, curly-headed boy, two octaves higher, as he busied himself with some task at the back of the studio.

The fat officer leaned back in his armchair. "Haven't you seen him, Pietro?" he asked the bull-necked man in a firm, youthful voice.

"Whom?"

"Why, the Archduke you were just enquiring about?"

"No!"

"I saw him at the Palace."

"Is he good-looking?"

"Why should he be good-looking?" said the fat officer, breathing heavily.

"Why—he's an Imperial Prince—and young—" replied Pietro, in broken snatches, absorbed in his modelling.

Not a muscle of the fat officer's face moved. "He looks like all the others," he said.

"What others?"

"The other princes of his House, of course."

"I don't know them," exclaimed Pietro peevishly.

"I know them all," was the calm rejoinder.

And breathing heavily, he leaned forward to paint.

The silence that ensued was broken by Cesare Bandini suddenly exclaiming, "And what do you want?"

But as he did not look up from his work, Lucas did not know that the words were addressed to him. All he noticed was that the fat officer stared at him and nodded twice. He stood there not knowing what to do until the officer raised his hand and pointed his brush at Bandini.

Pulling himself together Lucas stepped closer to the Maestro, picking his way carefully on tip-toe through the narrow openings between the easels, turn-tables, furniture and stools. When he was within a couple of paces of Bandini, he stopped. The Maestro did not turn round but went on painting.

"What do you want?" he asked after a while.

"I want to learn," murmured Lucas at the black brocade of the painter's back.

"What's your name?" enquired Bandini after another pause.

"Lucas Grassi."

"Was the stone-carver, Lucas Grassi, your father then?" asked Bandini immediately. He spoke slowly, but his speech sounded hesitating only because he was intent on his work.

"Yes," Lucas replied to the back.

"Dead?" enquired Bandini in lower tones.

"Yes," said Lucas even more softly.

"What made you come to me?"

"Agostino Cassano told me that I ought to come to you."

At the mention of Agostino's name Bandini gave a merry laugh and turned round. He was a tall man with a powerful, refined face, the ivory skin of his handsome features standing out from the sharp edge of his dark beard. Lucas noticed his rich black locks, streaked here and there with gray, surmounting a finely curved, eloquent brow. He saw two brown eyes alight with vital energy, kindness and genius gazing at him, and heard

the generous lips asking him with a smile of amusement: "Oh, Agostino Cassano–the dear old fool–how is
he getting on?"

"He was your pupil–he is hard at work–he's getting
on all right," replied Lucas eagerly.

He no longer felt embarrassed. He was carried away.
The love, the first spark of which had been kindled a
moment ago, now flared up into a flame of passion
for the man who stood calm and majestic before him,
friendly yet full of dignity, radiating the power of a
great will.

"What can you do?" Bandini enquired gently as his
expression became serious.

"Nothing."

"What do you want to learn?"

"Everything."

"Giuseppe!" cried Bandini in his sing-song voice.

The boy with the cherub's head hurried forward.

"Bring a drawing-board and some charcoal for
Lucas," said the Maestro, "and go and fetch the head
of Vulcan too. . . . Take a seat where you like and do

the best you can," he added, turning to Lucas.

So saying he turned back to his picture.

Lucas followed little Giuseppe. Behind a forest of easels a young monk was sitting. He had been hidden from Lucas, and as the latter found himself suddenly just in front of him, he stammered the usual greeting, "Praised be the Lord."–"Forever and ever, Amen. . . ." murmured the young monk, without looking up.

Giuseppe pointed to a place close beside him, pushed a small wooden drum forward and hurrying away again, returned with a drawing-board and some charcoal together with a bronze head of Vulcan wearing a cap. This he placed on the drum. Then he jumped up onto a little platform in front of the monk's easel, planted himself upon it and stood motionless. With astonishment Lucas noticed the boy's graceful and solemn pose, the enraptured look of his up-turned eyes; cautiously turning round, he saw that the monk at his side was painting a young John the Baptist, with Giuseppe as model.

Lifting the drawing-board onto his knee, Lucas

gazed steadily at the head of Vulcan, and immediately became absorbed in the ardent anxiety, joy, fear and hope of work.

He hardly heard the snatches of conversation which his entry had interrupted, and the exclamation "He's coming!" which someone shouted a moment later as he flung open the door, fell on deaf ears as far as he was concerned.

Even when, a moment later, the Archduke and his suite entered the studio, he scarcely noticed them. The glittering figure of the Prince as he wandered round with Count Waltersburg, fat old Pointner and the rest of his little retinue, fell on his eye as a picture in the dim distance. They were nothing to him now. They did not concern him.

As the days slipped by Lucas gradually became aware that a change was coming over the spell under which he had reached Florence. When the moment of trans-formation came he was no longer hurled back into the Prince's stables.

As long as the journey had lasted, he had been able, on the days when he was allowed to be himself, to go wherever he pleased; he might remain lying down in the road, or run back along the way he had come, or wander about as he chose. But the traveling party to which he was attached as a dog took possession of him night after night, the moment the hour of his bondage struck, and either dragged him along with it or flung him in the straw at the horses' feet.

But here in Florence when the transformation occurred it left him on the spot where he happened to be standing or walking at the time.

Lucas had not paid overmuch attention to this during his first night in the city. On the following day also the change occurred without his being conscious of it. He had spent the day in Bandini's studio, engaged on the wretched probationary task of drawing the head of Vulcan, and what with this and the Maestro's promise that he might count on remaining his pupil, he had left the place aflame with dreams and hopes. Thus he had wandered about until the hour of midnight rang out and he was struck by the lightning that shattered all his lofty visions. Whereupon, leaving the place where he had been standing, and guided by his unerring sense of smell, he ran in the shape of a tired dog direct to the Palace, found his way to the stable, and, after discovering a crack through which he could steal in, dropped into the straw and fell fast asleep.

On another day, however, as he was leaving Bandini's house at about twilight with the intention of strolling down to the banks of the Arno to get a breath of fresh air, he happened to hear the agonized howls of a dog close at hand. His heart constricted so violently that he was afraid he must have burst a blood vessel. He ran forward breathless. The howling grew louder and louder and sounded as though it came from a neighboring alley. He hastened on and, as he turned a corner, saw a youth thrashing a skinny black dog with a chain. The dog was writhing in agony on the ground. Every time it tried to get up a fresh blow made it fall back exhausted. Lucas could hear the harrowing appeal in the howl of the wretched animal as its heart-rending wails died down into a bitter whine. He was beside himself with fury. With one jerk of his arm he seized the youth, lifted him off his feet and turning him about so as to see his face, proceeded to punch him heavily in the jaw. Dazed and staggered, the fellow flung out at him with the chain. He was a powerful man but Lucas hurled him like a rag against the wall, and making a dash for his throat, held it in such a tight grip that he went blue in the face. He might have throttled him had not a couple of watchmen hurried up and separated the pair.

Lucas was raving like a maniac, and the youth, gasping for breath and wiping the blood from his swollen nose, swore that he had been assaulted without the slightest provocation. Seeing that Lucas was a stranger to the city, the watchman, like the youth, took him to be a robber, and dragged him away to prison, where he was thrust into a dark cell. The youth, who said he was Tommaso the bricklayer, was instructed to appear in court on the following morning to charge the prisoner. But early the next day, when the jailer opened the cell to fetch Lucas, the dog, which everybody knew to be the Archduke's, sprang out. Utterly taken aback by the mystery, and terrified in case an enquiry were made into the matter and he were punished, the man quickly let the dog go. Evidently it must have slipped into the cell in some unaccountable way without his noticing it, and all he reported to the authorities was that the young stranger who had been arrested had vanished as if by magic.

At about this time it struck Lucas that the spell that lay on him was indeed beginning to weaken a little. On waking up soon after midnight to find that he was himself again, he got up and made for the Poggio pine woods on the hills. The darkness was slowly lifting though Lucas hardly noticed the fact. He was used to such excursions and was brooding over his fate. The constant humiliation of being repeatedly banished from the society of his fellows made him intolerably wretched, though at the same time he could not forget that it was precisely this humiliation that had brought him where he was and had made it possible for him to be in Florence working under Cesare Bandini.

It did seem, however, as if certain changes were taking place. Now, even when debased and humiliated he went about as a dog, he was free, and was no longer forced to be with his princely master or in his house or stable. Whatever the form he wore, whether his own or that of his doglike poverty, the decision as to his whereabouts seemed to lie with himself. He had reached his goal; the noose about his neck had begun to slacken—how he did not know.

Suddenly an idea occurred to him—what if he were to run away from Florence and go to Rome! In Rome too he would be able to find masters to teach him to paint and carve. And another thought surged madly in his brain—if the spell were not removed so that he could be a free man, he might throw himself at the feet of the Pope. The Pope might have the power to release him from the spell!

He halted. He was quivering with breathless excitement, so violently did his spirit rebel against his fate. But sadly he remembered that this would mean parting from Cesare Bandini which he was loath to do. His passionate boyish love of Bandini lifted its voice and, tearing to shreds the web of plans he had just woven, immediately suggested all kinds of doubts and objections. Why go away? Had he not everything he had coveted here? And though the spell still kept fast hold on him, the Pope would be unable to liberate him from it for he would never be able to reach Rome or see the Pope. The same thing would happen as had happened on the journey from Vienna. He would find himself a day's march from Florence only to be hurled back again at midnight and returned to wherever the Archduke was staying. Again and again he would try to do that day's march only to find himself again and again at midnight back at the place from which he had set out. So why go away?

But what would happen on the day the Archduke left Florence? The thought struck him like a thunderbolt. It acted like an elixir, making the blood run hot in his veins, and rose light as a falcon beating the air with its wings. On the day when the Archduke began his homeward journey would he be dragged along with him and forced to return to Vienna? No—that would be absurd, impossible! As a man buried alive sees in the distance from the depths of his premature grave the first ray of light breaking through beneath the spades of his rescuers, so Lucas now looked forward to the Archduke's departure as the only possible means of release from his terrible predicament. He laughed. No! No! When the Archduke went home, he would be free, free as air, and his nightmare would end.

He looked about him. The day had grown brighter. The tree tops were rustling in the morning breeze. He began to run, leaping and dancing as he left the confines of the wood. At last he reached the walls of the monastery of Fiesole and looked down on Florence at his feet, lying bathed in the glory of the morning sun.

"Have you made friends with him yet?"

Cesare Bandini was sitting on the fat officer's armchair as he asked the question. He spoke quietly, glancing over at Lucas, who was sitting some distance away by the side of the monk, absorbed in his work.

Captain Ercole da Moreno, the fat officer, was standing behind Bandini, as excited and modest as a young pupil, watching the Maestro with fevered brow and his mop of white hair almost standing up on end as his teacher criticised and corrected the little Madonna picture. Short, bull-necked Pietro Rossellino also left his turn-table and joined them. Cesare Bandini inclined his head this way and that, screwed up his eyes, and touched the picture here and there with his fine pointed brush, humming softly to himself. The two pupils stood behind his chair, watching in intent silence. Captain Ercole was breathing heavily. Now and again Bandini said a word or two. "Yes . . . that's all right. . . ." or "What about this fold here . . . you meant it to look like that, didn't you?" And Ercole da Moreno would give a loud snort. "The expression should be a little more serene, Ercole," Bandini continued. "It's all in the eyes . . . and here in the cheeks. You'll get it right in time."

"Oof!" gasped the Captain.

Presently Bandini leaned back in the arm-chair, and

glancing across at Lucas again, whispered: "Have you made friends with him yet?"

"He's been once or twice to the osteria with us, yes," replied Pietro Rossellino.

"And what do you make of him?" asked Bandini, leaning back in the chair and glancing up enquiringly at the Captain.

"A good fellow!" replied Ercole.

"Yes, I like him," Bandini observed with a smile. "He works like one possessed. He plays with his task like a child, grapples with it like a man, and thinks of nothing else. At least, when he's at his easel, he has the strength to forget everything else."

"But has he genius?" Rossellino exclaimed peevishly.

Bandini smiled. "Just look at him, Pietro, and tell me how he could possibly fail to have genius. I want to paint him—or rather I want to teach him to paint himself. It will be a picture worthy of taking its place by the side of the best great masters' portraits of themselves as young men. At all events I for one can never look at him without thinking—the portrait of a great master as a young man. . . ."

"It sounds all right, Bandini," said Ercole, shaking his great mane of hair. "You may be right . . . I don't understand enough about it."

"Why, the man has his calling written all over his drawn features," exclaimed Bandini. "He's all will, one single thought breathes from every pore. Have you ever looked into his eyes? What a powerful soul, what a potent spirit lies hid in them! But it is impossible to read them. They reveal nothing, those eyes of his—nothing either about his soul or his spirit. All they do is to absorb, devour the whole world about them; they pilfer everything they rest on."

"Thief!" snorted Ercole.

"Ye-es," chanted Bandini, with a contented little laugh. "Every man who conquers the world is a thief. But he pays her back two or three times over at compound interest, so that after all he is a prince. That fellow is only just beginning, and that's why today he is still a beggar. Later on he too will be a prince. He does not know it. Yet he is half aware of it. He is burning with the desire to become what he will be in time. Just you watch him. He looks poor and weak and wretched, doesn't he? But he has the iron thinness of the man fighting with Fate, the man who will do or die! What a brave, proud nose he has! Do you notice how slender it is at the root and thin between the eyes? The height of the bridge is exactly right, and it stands out with noble determination. What do you think, Pietro? I don't know, but I almost feel as if the feature I like best about him is his mouth."

"Too small," whispered Pietro.

"Possibly," replied Bandini, describing figures in the air with his finely shaped hand, as though his attention were focussed on some picture. "Possibly. All the same . . . his mouth . . . his mouth . . . what does its expression signify? Those fine lips do not breathe, they imbibe. They are silent and yet seem always as if they must speak. They are insatiable. God in Heaven! how frantically eager that mouth is for life!"

"What one would like to know," snorted Ercole,

"what one would like to know is whether he has ever kissed a woman."

"Why don't you ask him if you want to know so badly?" laughed Bandini, unexpectedly rising from his seat. And a sudden shadow passed across his face as he once more glanced over at Lucas. "Well, we'll see how he turns out," he remarked in a changed voice as he returned to his own easel.

Presently the garden door was flung open, and Filippo Volta, the man who had introduced Lucas on his first visit to the studio, appeared on the threshold.

"Claudia is here!" he cried gleefully. "She wants to know whether she may come in."

"Ye-es," replied a sing-song voice from behind Bandini's easel.

Filippo Volta hesitated. "I only ask because she happens to have Count Peretti with her. . . ."

Bandini did not reply and after a moment Filippo Volta vanished. Outside the sound of a woman laughing could be heard, together with a confused murmur of voices and the rustle of skirts.

A little knot of people pressed through the garden door and scattered, allowing a tall young woman to step proudly forward.

Deeply moved by her appearance, Lucas turned quickly to the monk who was sitting beside him. "Reverend brother—who is that?" he stammered in low tones.

But the monk, who had already sprung to his feet, left the place without vouchsafing a reply.

A rude and blustering man's voice could suddenly be heard asserting itself. "Just look at Claudia, Bandini! Yesterday I bought the pearls she has in her hair and only an hour ago I bought the cloak she is wearing. We want to know what you think of them."

"Silence, you idiot!" exclaimed Claudia sharply. "Can't you wait until you're asked?"

Everybody laughed, even Count Peretti joining in. He stood there fat and conceited, his brutal face with its massive chin thrust forward, and his sharp little eyes screwed up. Utterly at a loss to know what to say or do, he merely looked knowing and laughed.

"Bandini," observed Claudia, "I have not come about the pearls or the stupid cloak.... I wanted to see you and enjoy the pleasure of your company again." Her voice sounded gentle, almost tender, with a proud golden ring in it, vibrating with joy and expectation.

Bandini went on painting.

Lucas gazed in utter bewilderment at the young woman. Her blue velvet cloak, embroidered with silver lilies, hung in heavy, luxurious folds from her slender shoulders, enveloping her frame like solemn music, while the broad sweep of its ermine border was held up behind by the hands of a little Moorish servant, who stood stiff and motionless behind her, allowing only the whites of his eyes to move. Lucas gazed spellbound at the gold brocade and white lace which hardly hid her breast; he noticed the edging of soft downy fur tenderly encircling her dazzling white neck, and on the latter he saw the tiny curls which seemed almost to breathe. He saw her hair shimmering with the pearls entwined in its meshes and crowning her lovely face like a helmet of gold, and he caught the proud and happy glance in her sparkling blue eyes.

"May I look at what you are painting, Bandini?" she asked. "I haven't been here for such a long time."

Bandini made some reply in his sing-song voice and went on painting. Claudia came closer. But suddenly drawing herself up, she turned to Peretti, who was pressing after her. "What do you want?" she asked sternly.

Peretti gave a loud guffaw. "Just listen, Bandini, she is asking what I want! Just as if I didn't want to see your picture, too!"

"Don't make such a noise in here, you idiot!" snapped Claudia. "It's quite impossible to bring you into decent company. . . . Hold your tongue, I tell you!" And she repeated her orders even more sharply, when Peretti tried to laugh. "Bandini never gave you permission to look at his picture," she added.

Peretti had retreated a step or two. "Bandini," he cried, "what do you say to that? She says you haven't given me permission!"

Bandini did not reply at once. But presently, without

interrupting his work, he said calmly, "Perhaps you will have an opportunity of seeing the picture when it is finished." His tone was cheerful and courteous but his words seemed to fix a great gulf between himself and Peretti.

For a moment the studio was plunged in silence, the only sound that could be heard being the puffing and blowing of Captain Ercole behind his little Madonna picture.

"Bandini, I'll buy your picture!" cried Peretti. "I'll buy it as it stands, and give it to Claudia. How much do you want for it? I'll buy it on the spot. . . . I don't even wish to see it."

He spoke with great excitement, a note of anger lurking in his words; but he made no attempt to get closer. He turned to Claudia's two young female servants as he spoke, and to the fat old mulatto who was standing beside the Moorish boy, and then glanced round the studio expectantly to see what impression his offer had produced.

"Aren't you going to stop blustering and swaggering

about like a mountebank, you lout?" exclaimed Claudia, turning to him with an impatient laugh. She was now standing behind Bandini's easel.

"Come, Claudia," said Bandini when silence had been restored, "your way of addressing Peretti is new to me."

"It is not my way, but his," laughed Claudia. "It's the way which suits him; it is only what he deserves."

Bandini smiled.

"Yes," Claudia went on gravely and simply, "ever since he was a child the fellow has always been addressed as my lord this and my lord that, and may it please your lordship, and heaven knows what other tomfoolery. . . . It is too ridiculous . . . an idiot like him! It's high time he learned that he is a blockhead, a booby, an absolute buffoon and nothing else. He must be told it once and for all. The information is long overdue. . . . Oh, you leave it to me, Bandini, he is only getting what he deserves."

"Oh, I'm not objecting," replied Bandini with a smile.

"No! That's all right!" cried Claudia in high glee.

"Do you suppose he does not know he is only

getting what he deserves?" she asked presently in grave, eager tones. "And he takes it well from me. He likes it. The fool does not understand what I mean, and that's why he enjoys it. A man like him imagines he is something quite different, if you please—above everything and everybody!"

Peretti gave a derisive laugh.

"Hush!" cried Claudia angrily. "You have no idea, Bandini," she continued, "what liberties a fellow like that has the impudence and presumption to take! The things he has done already! Oh, it's not the least bit of good calling him a blockhead, a lout, an idiot and God knows what else. He should be made to feel—yes, feel—that there is someone stronger, than he is. Good heavens! if only some man could come along—some man who would knock him down with one blow!"

Lucas was twitching with longing to fulfill the wish of the fair Claudia on the spot. He was seized with a mad courage, a blessed madness. As he sprang to his feet his drawing-board fell to the ground with a crash. He almost fell down himself. But he came to his senses almost immediately. Claudia had looked at him!

Standing between the two maids, Peretti was laughing coarsely and winking at the mulatto.

"Well, did you hear what I said, Bandini," he cried quite unconcerned, "I'll buy that picture. . . ."

Once again Bandini allowed a few moments to elapse, and then in calm and distant tones, replied: "The picture belongs to his Grace the Archduke."

"Oh really!" interposed Claudia gleefully. "That woman there on the triumphal car—Victory or whoever she is—the more I look at her—surely she's meant for me!"

"Certainly," replied Bandini, "she is not unlike you in many ways. . . ."

"From memory!" Claudia exclaimed in astonishment. "Did you actually paint me from memory?"

"Of course!"

"How lovely to think that you remember me so well!" she continued with a sweet smile. "How delightful of you, Bandini. But—why didn't you send for me? Wouldn't that have been better?"

"No!"

"Why not?"

"I did not need you."

Claudia's gentle laugh rippled through the room. "But how silly of you, Bandini. You wanted to paint me, and yet you did not need me . . . no, really, Bandini, you are silly although you are such a dear! So you did not need me . . . can you explain that to me?"

"No!"

"You see, you can't even explain it to me. And why not?"

"Because you would not understand, Claudia."

"But explain it all the same," she begged, suddenly dropping into caressing tones, and imploring him humbly and gently. "Please do, I shan't leave you a moment's peace until you have explained."

"I wanted, Claudia, to paint you as you might be," was Bandini's mild rejoinder. "That is why I did not need you, that is why I did not wish to have you here in person. Do you understand?"

Claudia hesitated. "I . . . don't know," she replied. "I

hate that picture!" she added with a sudden revulsion of feeling.

Bandini took no notice of the remark. He continued calmly, "But I should like to paint a study of you now, and your visit happens to be extremely opportune."

"Really?" cried Claudia, recovering her good cheer. "Do you want to paint me? How lovely! Do you really want to paint me? Now at once?"

"I want to paint your bust," replied Bandini. "So will you be so good as to undress?"

"Peppina! Carletta!" cried Claudia excitedly, and began hurriedly trying to unfasten her tight-fitting bodice.

The maids came forward and Peretti with them. "Oh," he said with a laugh, "if you want to paint Claudia's bust you must ask my permission and allow me to be present!"

"Am I your slave, Alessandro," exclaimed Claudia, drawing herself up.

"But I must be present!" stammered Peretti, taken aback by her haughtiness.

"You will just go into the garden while I'm sitting," replied Claudia, "and you will take Caligula and Hassan with you," she added, pointing to the mulatto and the Moor. "Please be quick!" she whispered to Peppina and Carletta, who were unfastening her dress, and she took no further notice of Peretti.

Peretti was seething with indignation. "But surely I must be present!" he protested, turning his sledgehammer chin to Bandini as if he would fain crush the artist to powder.

The Maestro returned his look. "There are only workers in this studio," he replied gently, "and no spectators."

"But I—" roared Peretti, interrupting him.

"You will go into the garden," said Bandini, as if he had not heard his last remark, "and you will take those two fellows with you."

While his voice sounded soft and indifferent, his brown eyes flashed forth a command which brooked no resistance.

Peretti turned sharply round. "Come along, Caligula,"

he hissed to the old mulatto. "Go ahead, Hassan!" And giving the little Moor a kick, he looked round for the door. "To hell with the lot of them!" he muttered under his breath. "As far as I am concerned," he added a little louder, "they can all go to hell!" As he passed Captain Ercole who was leaning back in his arm-chair looking at him, he roared: "I don't care a straw!" and banged the glass door with a crash behind him.

Claudia, stripped to the waist, had taken her stand on the little platform. There had been no need to tell her what to do; she had immediately assumed the attitude of the figure in the picture. Peppina and Carletta were sitting on the steps of the platform, singing a song to the strains of a lute and chattering together as Bandini painted.

Lucas held his drawing-board motionless on his knees. He was blind to everything except Claudia's shining golden head, and her slightly raised figure. The minutes flew by. He did not notice Bandini step back from his easel, or little Giuseppe dash forward to pick up the brushes the artist had flung aside and set to work to wash them. All he knew was that Claudia was stretching out her arms, and relaxing her body, her breast heaving as she breathed.

"Who is that stranger over there? I do not know him," she said. Lucas did not understand that she was referring to him, and was conscious only of the melody of her sweet, proud voice. But a moment later he heard himself being called by name, and started up terrified.

"Lucas!" cried Bandini.

He stood up, but seemed to be rooted to the spot.

Again he heard, "Lucas!" and Bandini made a friendly sign to him. He staggered forward, pale as death, his eyes still fixed on Claudia. "This is Lucas Grassi," said Bandini. "He hasn't been with me very long, but we are very good friends."

Lucas felt encouraged by the words which enabled him to meet more steadily the scrutiny of Claudia's dazzling blue eyes.

"He is still a stranger here in Florence," Bandini continued. "I hand him over to your charge, Claudia."

She stepped down with a smile from the platform

and stood so close to Lucas that he could breathe in the fragrance of her neck and shoulders.

"Why he's a mere boy," she murmured softly.

Her maids dressed her, while Bandini watched the scene with folded arms. Lucas did not stir.

"I hope you will all dine with me to-night," said Claudia, as her maids fastened her bodice. "Will you come too, Lucas Grassi?"

She waited a moment for a reply, "Why, he doesn't even answer," she said, in scoffing tones, turning to Bandini.

"Oh, he'll come," Bandini replied with a smile. "He answered you all right, and you read his answer quite plainly."

She shrugged her shoulders and turned away. Then going up to Bandini, she stopped, threw her arms round his neck and whispered shyly, "I suppose I mayn't hope that you will come yourself?"

"To-night I have to be at the Palace," he replied courteously, meeting her gaze with calm composure.

She bowed her head, but immediately raised her

face to his. "Good-bye," she said, very softly, and waited.

Bending down to her, Bandini kissed her on the mouth, and she quickly left the studio.

The cherub immediately busied himself about the place. Ercole da Moreno had gone out with Claudia, and Rossellino had also vanished. Lucas, back in his place again, was holding his drawing-board on his knee and gazing into space.

Bandini, who was pacing slowly up and down, suddenly came to a standstill in front of him. "Where is brother Serafio?" he enquired, pointing to the monk's empty chair.

Lucas had to think a moment before he could remember. "He left when . . . when Monna Claudia came in," he replied.

"As usual," Bandini observed with a nod, "of course I had forgotten."

"That he had to go?" cried Lucas. He did not understand.

Bandini gazed into the distance. "Yes, he has to go when she comes. . . . She is his sister."

"His sister?" cried Lucas, staring at the Maestro.

Bandini turned away, and began pacing up and down again. Lucas was thinking of the monk, and suddenly felt unaccountably drawn to him.

"Listen, Lucas," said Bandini, coming up to him, and laying a hand on his shoulder. "Listen, my son ... what is the matter with you?"

Lucas jumped to his feet and returned Bandini's gaze without flinching. He did not understand what he meant, and waited in silent expectation.

"You are a most zealous pupil, Lucas," continued Bandini kindly, though there was a touch of severity underlying his words. "You learn quickly and easily; your eyes are good and your hands are skillful. . . . I suppose I ought to be pleased with you. . . ."

Lucas closed his eyes and smiled, as though he were being stroked.

"What's more, you seem to be a good fellow," Bandini went on, "and yet you stop away so often and one sees nothing of you. You disappear! You are here one day and work hard, and one imagines that you are pleased to be allowed to come, and then the next day you are absent again."

Lucas hid his face in his hands.

"What is the matter with you?" Bandini repeated. "What do you do with yourself? What am I to think?"

Lucas groaned. His shoulders heaved, as if shaken by a sob, which he held in and stifled. Bandini waited a moment.

"Can't you tell me?" he asked tentatively after a while.

Lucas shook his head.

Bandini gazed at him for some moments. "Very well," he said, "very well, it is a secret. You do not strike me as being a fellow who would be up to silly larks . . . and still less would you be capable of anything mean," he added in lower tones.

Quickly taking his hands from his face, Lucas looked into Bandini's eyes. "I can't tell you," he muttered, "not today anyhow. . . ." He was pale as death.

Bandini gazed into his agonized face and into the depths of his imploring eyes. "All right," he said, nodding kindly, "don't worry, my son. I sha'n't ask any more questions."

And he withdrew.

On the great square in front of the monastery of San Marco Lucas chanced to pass the osteria where he often spent his evenings with the other students. His footsteps had led him that way from sheer force of habit. The conversation with Bandini had perturbed him so much that he had left the studio quite unable to think clearly and had abandoned himself to despair without a struggle.

Ercole da Moreno and Pietro Rossellino were sitting together on a bench in front of the osteria. On a flap let down between them stood some bottles of wine and some glasses.

"Now then, don't pass us by with your head in the clouds!" cried the Captain.

At the sound of the gruff cheery voice, Lucas looked up and stopped just in front of Ercole. With a sense of relief he awoke from his reverie and for the first time it came home to him what torture his solitude had been.

"Have a drink!" said Ercole kindly, proffering a glass of wine. Lucas looked at him. His ruddy face, full of courage and good cheer, on which the hand of time had left its mark, though it was still fresh and vigorous, the severity of his features, particularly of his white mustache and his bushy white eyebrows, and his mild and gentle smile—this face, so eloquent of friendship and simple trust and confidence, soothed and comforted Lucas. Taking the glass he drained the contents at one gulp.

"So you are going to Claudia today?" said Ercole.

The sound of the name was like a fresh breath of life to Lucas.

"But I don't know where she lives," he replied.

Pietro Rossellino shrugged his shoulders derisively.

"Any child could show you the way," he observed.

"We are all going to her place," added Ercole with a laugh, "so come along with us." He hummed a melody under his breath.

The immediate prospect of seeing Claudia again

suddenly filled Lucas with fresh courage and hope
and he felt convinced that the day would surely come
when he would be free and his real self again forever.
The conviction once more took a firm grip on his
mind.

"Who is Claudia?" he asked. "I do not know her."

"Claudia is Claudia," growled Pietro Rossellino.

The Captain stopped humming. "You saw today
who she is," he replied slowly, turning his flashing eyes
to Lucas. "Besides, you've only to set eyes on her to know
at once who she is, haven't you?"

Pietro Rossellino gave a short laugh and threw his
head back. "Claudia can do as she likes. All her sins will
be atoned for over there," he added, pointing to the
monastery across the square.

"Over there?"

"Of course! Brother Serafio, who sits next to you—
but don't you know?"

"She is his sister," replied Lucas. "What else is there
to know?"

"He went into the monastery for her sake," replied

Rossellino in sullen, serious tones. "On the very day that Claudia became a courtesan!"

The Captain sprang to his feet. "You low, coarse brute, Rossellino," he exclaimed in his rich, deep bass. "You are a boor, and a boor you will remain to the end of your days." He stared hard at Rossellino. "Do you know what Serafio said when he went into the monastery? He said 'I must get into the other side of the scales!' Do you understand what that means?"

"And why should I not understand?" replied Rossellino, wiping the wine from his lips, his head on one side.

"Because you are a boor," said the Captain calmly. "A good fellow, but a boor. What a fine chap that Serafio is! He used always to sit by me, over there in the studio and here in the osteria and heaven knows where else! Whether he was at work, drinking, or in the company of women, he always had fire, youth—he was splendid! And then, when that business with his sister happened, he said, 'I must get into the other side of the scales.' I asked him what he meant and he said, 'It can't go on like this. We can't both have a good time, both my sister and I.' 'Why not, Tonio?' I asked. 'Why should not both of you have a good time?' 'Not in that way!' he replied. 'What one enjoys the other must pay for. It can't be helped, I saw that at once!' He had suddenly changed, as though his light had gone out, and he was shut up inside himself like a tower. 'She must live a life for us both,' he said, 'and I will serve God for us both.' And on the next day he was over there." Ercole pointed to the monastery. His face was aflame, his lips smiled under his white mustache. "Fine!" he cried, turning to Lucas. "Fine, wasn't it?" Then, gazing into the distance, he added, "But Tonio was mistaken. There is no need for anyone to atone for Claudia. Even so it was a fine idea all the same!"

"But, after all," he continued, his face lighting up, "it is better to have no sister, and to enjoy oneself with other people's sisters! Eh? Let's go to Claudia!"

And they sauntered slowly along through the streets in the twilight as the full moon rose in the clear evening sky. Ercole da Moreno was singing softly to himself.

Claudia's house stood in a narrow, quiet and deserted little street. They knocked at the door and as they stood waiting outside they could hear the din of voices, the clatter of crockery, and the sound of laughter mingling with the music. From the dim twilight of the badly lighted hall they entered the dining-room, which was a blaze of candlelight. Lucas saw the gleaming white stretch of table as it were through a veil, and the various figures round it seemed just as dim. But when his eyes fell on Claudia, he was spellbound. She was seated in a great thronelike chair, upholstered in red velvet, with gold borders. Her silk dress which left her shoulders bare was a dark blue. A large sapphire hung from the golden chain about her neck, and lay sparkling on her bare breast.

She had been laughing and talking, but as soon as Lucas entered and remained standing at the door, she suddenly became silent, looked gravely across at him, with a quick searching glance, and greeting him kindly, turned away.

Lucas felt a touch on his arm. It was Filippo Volta.

The young man accosted him in the same friendly, slightly curious way he had done in the hall of Bandini's house on the first day they had met, and with the same readiness to help. "Come with me," he said, "there's a place for you over there." And leading him to the table, he set him down on an upholstered seat. Lucas found himself at the far end of the table from Claudia, but facing her. She was such a long way off, however, that he felt at ease, knowing that neither she nor any of the others would notice him.

He could hear Alessandro Peretti's loud laugh, and was surprised to see Count Waltersburg sitting by Claudia. The little Moor with the white turban was standing behind Claudia's chair. The mulatto, Caligula, was giving orders and calmly superintending the banquet. Fat and lazy, he leaned against the sideboard, his observant, squinting eyes wandering restlessly round the room, as though he were maliciously listening to every word. Peppina and Carletta tripped backward and forward round the table waiting on the guests. Peppina, who was fourteen and had just blossomed into womanhood, looked round as though she had just heard something extremely diverting which she was longing to discuss.

Two or three other servants glided swiftly hither and thither, while the humble strains of the musicians seated in a recess were almost drowned by the buzz and clamor of the guests. The air was filled with the sound of people talking at the tops of their voices, a babel of shouting and chatter, while above it rose occasional bursts of laughter. The room reeked of burning candles, the fumes of wine and viands, the fragrances of flowers and the scent of clothes.

"Do you see that old fellow over there?" Filippo Volta asked Lucas, "The wizened little man with the bald head—yes, that one! He is sitting next to the stranger from Austria. That is Giovanni Belloni, the old wool-merchant. Have a good look at him. He is fabulously rich, is old Belloni, and has possessed the most beautiful women."

Lucas looked across at the little old man with his pale face and his hollow, toothless jaws. He was sitting quietly there, taking long, slow drafts of wine, and leaning back with his eyes closed as though he were asleep.

"And you see that man in green over there," Filippo Volta went on. "That's Cosimo Rubinardo, whom Claudia ruined," he explained with a laugh.

Lucas looked across at a commanding figure of a man, dressed in green velvet trimmed with lace. He had a noble face with a lofty brow, a fine nose and gentle eyes, and seemed to be engrossed in conversation with two young noblemen.

"Cosimo Rubinardo," proceeded Filippo Volta, "belongs to one of our leading aristocratic families and was at one time very rich. He had property in Venice, and this house used to belong to him. He squandered everything on Claudia. She lets him live here in an attic now, and he is happy because he is allowed to be under the same roof with her."

And Filippo laughed loudly. "Count Peretti is going the same way," he continued. "He is ruining himself for Claudia, but she only laughs at him and will send him flying to the devil without mercy the moment she has extracted his last ducat. As for that fat fellow there—"

But Lucas was no longer listening. He had seen Peretti clutch Claudia with his clumsy hands, and Claudia shake him off so that he fell backward into his chair. An expression of wild despair and longing suffused his coarse, flushed face in which suspicion and incipient anger could be read, and a desire to escape from his torture by regarding it all as a joke. His massive chin was thrust violently forward, and he was squinting horribly. Claudia almost emptied a glass of wine and swinging it at Peretti flung the dregs in his face. This immediately restored his good-temper. He burst into loud guffaws of laughter, seized her hand, and covered her wrist with kisses. But Claudia turned to Count Waltersburg, who with a smile of amusement was whispering something in her ear.

Lucas turned his eyes to Captain Ercole da Moreno, who had just brought his goblet down on the table with a thundering crash. He looked magnificent as he sat there, animated by the wine and his enjoyment of the banquet, and though he was as calm as a statue, he sparkled with life. His ruddy cheeks and powerful brow were flushed, and his shock of hair stood up on end like a mass of snow-white flames. The young men pressed toward him on either side, hailing his every word with joy, and reveling in the smile that lurked beneath his white mustache. A mood of infectious cheerfulness radiated from him and seemed to be exhaled from his powerful, gentle head with its shimmering white crown of hair. Claudia made a sign to him.

"Yes, he's a fine old boy, is the Captain," observed Filippo Volta, who had noticed Lucas gazing intently at him. "He's a fine old boy. But no one seems to know much about him. Often he behaves as though he were merely Bandini's pupil, a beginner who has taken up art as a whim. And then all of a sudden he produces work which is so masterly that it takes one's breath away. Claudia is wearing a gold ring which he carved and chased. It is a jewel of which even Cellini would not have been ashamed. Can you understand it? Nobody knows what the fellow is. We don't even know whether Ercole da Moreno is his real name. And God alone knows how old he is! Why he even knew Queen Christina during her stay in Rome. She was Queen of Sweden, I believe, though I wouldn't like to swear to it. They say he was once her lover. He has fought in many a war and has been to France, Spain, Germany and every other country under the sun. But he never talks about it. Oh, he's a gay old spark! No one can beat him at that game; the women are after him even today!"

For some moments Lucas had not been listening. An urgent longing had been kindled in his breast, how he knew not—an uncontrollable desire, an impelling force, which made him feel like bursting. Suddenly the cup of life, filled to the brim, seemed to have been thrust into his hands for him to drain to the dregs that very hour. He was trembling with pent-up energy.

At this moment the Captain began to sing, and the din and clamor round the table was immediately silenced. The musicians stopped playing and put away their instruments as though they would no longer be required, and at the sound of that glowing voice, the room seemed to grow brighter.

"Pray let me live right long, O Lord!
Pray leave me here below. . . ."

sang the Captain.

There he sat, erect and youthful, as though in the saddle, his head slightly raised, his eyes turned to the ceiling, his face aflame with deep and joyous reverence. The song filled his face, it was in his brow, it quivered in the thick tufts of his white eyebrows, even his flaming snow-white mane of hair seemed to be singing. In the warm richness of his voice lay the suggestion of strength which still had reserves it did not need to draw upon to be stronger than the rest. Blithely did the song soar above the heads of the company, gathering their good cheer to itself, carrying it along, leading it on. Every pulse in the room seemed to beat to the solemn rhythm:

"Pray let me live right long, O Lord!
Pray leave me here below!"

Several of the young men had risen from their seats
and were listening to the song standing. At its finish they
all crowded round the Captain, wild with enthusiasm;
but with his head still thrown back, Ercole da Moreno
remained quietly seated. Not daring to embrace him,
they fell on one another's necks all round the room.
Swearing eternal friendship, they drank to each other's
health; there was a great clinking of glasses and bursts of
merry laughter, but no one shouted or cheered merely
for the sake of making his own voice heard. For the
song was still hovering above them.

Claudia was trying to keep Peretti at arm's length.
In an access of tenderness he was pressing his atten-
tions upon her.

"No, not you!" she cried. Her voice could be heard
all over the room. "Not you!"

Peretti sank back in his arm-chair. "Well then
nobody at all!" he growled.

Claudia laughed loudly. "You fool!" she exclaimed, her voice sparkling with joy and pride. "You poor fool, do you really imagine it must be you or nobody? But I don't think so!" She laughed again. "There is one man who may kiss me . . . but as I have said already—not you!" And looking round, she laughed again. Her eye wandered to Count Waltersburg, then glided over to Cosimo, passing the whole company in review till it rested on Lucas. "That young man over there—he is the man I want to kiss me. I will allow him to, because he is so young and solitary here."

Lucas sat rooted to his chair, utterly dumbfounded. He would have died rather than go up before them all and kiss Claudia. He felt as though his soul had been laid bare and the most secret wish of his heart betrayed.

"You over there," cried Claudia across the table. "You over there. . . . What is your name? . . . Don't you understand? Come over here to me!"

Filippo Volta pushed Lucas forward. He stood up and with feet heavy as lead crept along behind the chairs of the other guests. The music had started again, there was a fresh buzz of conversation all round, and only one or two were paying any attention to what Claudia was doing. But as he went along Lucas heard the Captain say, "His name is Lucas Grassi."

With the air of one who has been let into a secret, Peppina urged him toward the table, close to Peretti's chair. He obeyed and stood in front of Claudia. She laughed as she looked up at him. "You may kiss me," she said. Lucas felt as though he were being whipped.

He bent slowly toward her, miserable and ill at ease. But suddenly growing grave, while her great blue eyes beamed radiantly on him, she laid an admonitory finger on his lips and whispered low, almost into his ear, "Not yet . . . you are right . . . not yet . . . later on, when they have all gone! Peppina will show you where. . . ." And pushing him gently from her, she turned aside.

"You haven't kissed him at all!" roared Peretti.

"No."

"What did you say to him then?"

"I told him that I should love to kiss him, but that I

did not dare to because of you, you savage, in case you killed both him and me. . . ."

Peretti doubled up with laughter.

Lucas returned to his place. He could still feel the warm touch of Claudia's fingers on his lips and the fragrance of her breath on his cheek, while the song still rang in his brain: "Pray let me live right long, O Lord!"

Someone touched him on the shoulder, and turning round, he saw Peppina tripping away from him and beckoning.

He rose slowly and followed her with faltering steps, afraid that the others might observe him. But no one took any notice. As he was leaving the room, he had to pass by the mulatto Caligula. Suddenly he found his wicked, fat, yellow face thrust into his, and felt that his small squinting eyes were venomously spying upon him. But Peppina was beckoning to him from outside and he hastened on. He passed along a cool stone corridor illumined only by the silvery light of the moon, and, breathing in the pure air, he came to his senses.

Peppina led him through a heavy oak door, which

opened and shut without making a sound, and they found themselves in the dark. Whereupon taking him by the hand, the girl put an arm round his waist and led him on. Crossing a soft carpet, they reached a second door. Peppina was clinging closely to Lucas, trying to dally, but as he made no response, she pushed open the door. A soft golden light poured down from a hanging lamp on to the large, gaily furnished room which lay revealed to their eyes.

The floor was spread with richly colored rugs, tapestries lined the walls, priceless cabinets in lacquer and marquetrie, with doors outspread like wings, laid bare the glories of their ornate interiors with their columns, niches and tabernacle work. Statues, bronze busts, carvings in gilded wood and marble stood out in the confused medley beneath the dim light, while the reflections cast in the great mirrors round the room held out a deceptive vista of endless chambers beyond. From the depths of an alcove, like a distant landscape lit up by the rays of the setting sun, gleamed a great white couch.

Going up to a smooth wall covered with Gobelin

tapestry, Peppina pulled a cord. The tapestry slowly parted, revealing lofty glazed doors. The soft moonlight poured in through the windows, while outside the garden lay gleaming like silver amid the deep black shadows of the pines.

"You must go out there," said Peppina. "Go and hide out there behind the bushes and wait."

Lucas tried to pass her, but she barred the way. "If you like I will come too and stay with you," she said gazing at him with her knowing sphinx-like smile. As Lucas was silent, she bowed her pretty head. "At any rate, it won't be very long now. Wait down there. You must wait until Claudia opens this door and comes out on to the terrace; then you can show yourself." She smiled at him, nodded and ran away.

Stepping out into the open air, Lucas found himself on a little terrace, paved with black and white stone, brightly illumined by the light of the moon. On the low balustrade stood stone vases ablaze with bright red azalias; a short broad flight of steps led down into the garden.

He stood in the pale moonlight with the faint rustling melody of the trees above his head, breathing in the fragrance of the flowers in the night air, utterly dazed by the events of the evening.

Suddenly the cathedral chimes rang out close by. Other bells joined the chorus, and as Lucas listened and counted, the joy that had filled his heart died away.

It was a quarter to twelve.

He waited. He did not want to stir from the place. Almost he felt himself strong enough to fight and overcome both time and destiny. For others the night was free; it lay rich and unfettered before them, merging happily into the life of another day. He pursed his sensitive lips, but no sound of lamentation escaped them, and, all resistance at an end, he resigned himself to his fate.

Slowly he descended the beautiful steps into the garden, followed the path between the shadow of the bushes, and stepped out of the moonlight into the blackness to meet his humiliation. He had just enough time to climb over the wall. Once more the cathedral chimes rang out;

he felt the familiar shock and a second later a moon-
struck dog with lowered head was running through the
deserted streets. On and on he went, hither and thither,
through the city of Florence, never resting.

Archduke Ludwig and his suite rode out through the
city gates at a brisk trot. Count Waltersburg was beside
him, while close behind came Niccolo Torricella, the
Chamberlain, and Ugolino Corsini, who often performed the duties of page. Master Pointner brought up
the rear with various grooms.

As soon as they reached the fields which, surrounded by sparse woodland, stretched out to the bank
of the Arno, the Archduke started his black horse off at
a canter, and was immediately followed by the others,
the troop presenting a gay spectacle as they careered
over the sward. The dog, with his slender body and
limbs, swept round the cavalcade like the wind, and,
darting ahead and describing wide circles, would return
to his place at the side of the black horse.

"If Your Imperial Highness is agreeable," suggested

Niccolo Torricella, raising his hat, "we might dismount here." He was a fine-looking man of about fifty years of age. The skin of his lined clean-shaven chin had a dark bluish tinge. His expression was unspeakably haughty and his eyes, which were always half-closed, seemed to gaze upon the world as if it were not worth the exertion of raising his lids. He spoke in a semi-audible, monotonous tone which gave the impression of complete indifference, entirely in keeping with the rest of his personality.

The Archduke reined in his horse and sprang from the saddle. Count Waltersburg came up smiling inanely as usual, and looking as though he were congratulating himself on a phenomenal success. Master Pointner, summoning a groom to help him down from the saddle, dropped heavily to the ground.

"Where?" inquired Torricella in bored tones, turning indolently to Ugolino Corsini.

Young Corsini, a boy of eighteen, fat-cheeked and ruddy, with an expression of constant stupefaction on his face, stretched out a hand. "Along the bank," he replied.

The Archduke went in the direction indicated. The gentlemen followed at a respectful distance on either side.

"I don't know whether she will be alone," Count Waltersburg began anxiously. "That fellow Peretti may be with her."

"He can be kicked out," replied Torricella coolly.

The Archduke was silent.

The dog, who had run on ahead, suddenly stopped, raised his head, pricked up his ears.

"There she comes!" cried Ugolino Corsini, looking about him with a bewildered air.

A group of people could be seen emerging from the woods. They dispersed as they reached the field and came toward the Archduke's party.

"That fellow Peretti is with her," observed Count Waltersburg, turning to the Archduke. "I thought as much!"

The Archduke raised his gaunt face, thrust forward his underlip disdainfully and looked to one side. Then he stopped and waited.

Claudia came toward him. Her tight-fitting silk dress was dazzling white in the sunlight.

"Look, Your Highness, what Cambyses is doing!" cried Waltersburg with a laugh. "Strange what a fuss the brute is making over Claudia. . . ."

"What a beautiful dog!" cried Claudia, as she came up, "and so friendly." She tried to catch him as he gamboled round in an attitude of devoted homage, giving little barks of delight.

"He is behaving as though he knew you," remarked the Archduke suspiciously.

"He is indeed!" rejoined Claudia with a laugh.

"Perhaps he does know you?" the Archduke enquired more sharply.

"How could he possibly know me?" she exclaimed in amusement.

"Well," continued the Archduke dubiously, "the brute disappears every other moment and no one knows where he goes."

Peretti had now come up and made a stiff bow to the company. Captain Ercole da Moreno followed slowly behind, while Peppina stood glancing with laughing eyes from one to the other, her pretty face seeming to say: "I know a thing or two!" A little further off stood Caligula, the mulatto.

Niccolo Torricella pointed carelessly to Peretti, without even looking at him. "This gentleman here, Your Imperial Highness," his apathetic voice was heard to say, "is Count Alessandro Peretti."

Peretti again bowed stiffly and was on the point of saying something. But the Archduke, not deigning to look at him, turned to the Captain.

"Were you not dining with us the other day?" he asked. "I seem to have met you before, in Madrid. Am I not right? At the Infanta's. I was only a child in those days."

Ercole da Moreno nodded, a smile, as usual, playing about his handsome ruddy face and dark eyes. He gave a military salute, holding out his hat at arm's length, but as he did so, he staggered and almost fell, as the dog, overjoyed at seeing him, ran between his legs.

"Cambyses!" cried the Archduke. The dog immediately

dashed back, and stood quivering with excitement. Boisterously wagging his tail from side to side, he stood in front of Claudia and the Captain, looking affectionately up at them.

"How do you come to know Cambyses?" the Archduke enquired suspiciously of the Captain.

"Your Grace," exclaimed Claudia, coming forward and interrupting, "I think I understand the dog. Cambyses, isn't he?—a lovely name." She was standing close to the Archduke, looking into his eyes as she spoke, as though they were alone. "I think I understand Cambyses. He is exceptionally intelligent, more intelligent than any dog I have ever known. Of course he does not know either the Captain or me, but he does know who is welcome to his master . . ." and she cast a quick disdainful glance at Count Peretti.

A faint flush slowly spread over the Archduke's gaunt cheeks. He was breathing through his mouth, with his face close to Claudia's, while a film seemed to spread over his watery blue eyes. "You are indeed very welcome to me," he said in a hoarse voice.

Although surrounded by their retinue the two were now to all intents and purposes alone. For the others held aloof so as not to overhear what the Archduke was whispering in Claudia's ear.

"What a magnificent dog!" exclaimed Peretti at the top of his voice to each of the gentlemen in turn. "What a perfectly wonderful dog! I have never seen such a dog in my life. I don't believe such a dog has ever been seen in Italy before!"

Niccolo Torricella was gazing beneath his bored half-closed lids toward the Arno while Ugolino glanced in stupefaction from Peretti to the dog and from the dog to Peretti. But the latter had no intention of holding his tongue. It was all too plain that he was trying to divert the attention of the party from the Archduke and Claudia and was doing his best to conceal the humiliation of his own presence among them.

"Where are such dogs to be found?" he enquired, turning to Count Waltersburg. "I should be extremely interested to know where your master got this beautiful dog."

"Cambyses comes from Russia," replied Waltersburg

with a polite and condescending smile at Peretti. "Possibly from Persia—I am not quite sure."

"Do call him, please. I should like to have a closer look at him."

"Cambyses!" cried Waltersburg. But the dog did not seem to have heard.

"Apparently he does not think much of you!" exclaimed Peretti with an ill-natured laugh.

Waltersburg lost patience. "Pointner!" he cried, turning toward the place where the horses were standing, "make the dog come here."

Pointner whistled, without approaching the Archduke, and brought the dog forward as soon as he had timidly obeyed his summons.

Clumsily Peretti began patting the dog's back. But with a snarl the animal raised his lip, making wrinkles in his nose, and showed his teeth in such a savage manner that Peretti stepped back terrified. Seeing the others smiling, he gave an embarrassed laugh. "Will he go into the water?" he asked, suddenly picking up a stick he found lying on the bank.

Waltersburg glanced at Pointner.

"I don't know," replied Pointner.

"Do make him fetch this stick out of the water!" begged Peretti.

Pointner took the stick and went down the side of the bank, calling the dog. But the animal refused to follow him.

"Fetch it, Cambyses! Fetch it!" cried Pointner, waving the stick. But the dog stood still, refusing to take any interest, while Pointner held the stick to his nose, spat on it and continued to wave it about.

"Well, throw it!" insisted Peretti.

And Pointner flung it far into the water. It flashed through the air, splashed down into the water, and floated slowly away with the current. The dog had craned his neck to watch the stick as it flew through the air, and then stood still on the edge of the bank, looking anxiously at it floating away. Pointner pushed him along, catching hold of his hind quarters and shoving him forward to drive him into the water; but the dog, stiffening his forepaws, resolutely refused to budge.

Casting dignity to the winds, Peretti lost his temper. "You let the dog make fools of you all!" he exclaimed, slapping his thigh.

"Fetch it, Cambyses!" cried Pointner angrily.

"Such a huge dog and frightened of going into an inch of water!" cried Peretti scornfully. "It's ridiculous!"

"You damned rascal, go in, will you!" growled Pointner.

"Seize him by the scruff of the neck and fling him in!" roared Peretti.

Waltersburg waved toward the place where the horses were standing and two grooms hurried up.

The dog was lying flat on the ground. Pulling him up roughly, they swung him like a sack and flung him far into the river. He turned a somersault, saw the world about him—the river, the bank, the people on it, and everything—turn round and round, and was suddenly swallowed up as he fell in a dark, gurgling abyss. He struck out with his paws, rose to the surface, and swam, but was carried away by the current. Nevertheless, dazed though he was, terrified out of his wits, and struggling for breath, he managed to reach the bank. He clambered exhausted up the slope, shook himself, sending a cloud of spray flying all round him, and dropped shivering on the grass.

"Again!" shouted Peretti, "do it again! He didn't bring the stick back!"

The grooms were just going to fetch the dog, who was lying a little way off, at the spot where he had come ashore, when Ercole da Moreno called out, "No, that will do!"

Everybody looked round at him, but Peretti went on shouting and blustering: "Quick, over there! What are you staring at? Quick, run . . . ! Throw him in again!"

"No, that will do!" repeated the Captain calmly.

"He shall bring back that stick! I insist!" spluttered Peretti, his thick neck bulging with indignation.

The Captain glanced at him without turning his head.

"Quick! That stick! I insist!" cried Peretti, his voice growing louder as his anger rose.

"Go and fetch it yourself!" The words were calm

204 🦌 FELIX SALTEN

enough, but the tone in which they were uttered was low and fierce.

"What did you say, Moreno?" exclaimed Peretti, whisking round sharply and making a dash at the Captain. What little serenity he had left had vanished. He was purple in the face.

Count Waltersburg watched the two men with polite interest. Niccolo Torricella turned apathetically away, while an expression of stupefaction spread over young Ugolino Corsini's fat face.

"What did you say, Moreno?"

The Captain looked down at Peretti. There was an angry flash in the eyes beneath the bushy white eyebrows.

"I say that will do! . . . for the last time!" Suddenly turning pale to the lips, Peretti gave a short laugh and left the spot without wishing anyone farewell.

Brother Serafio stopped painting. In front of him, on the platform, stood the cherubic boy who was posing as a model for the youthful John the Baptist. But the monk was looking at Lucas, who was sitting beside him, lost in thought. After he had looked at him for a few minutes in silence, Brother Serafio went on painting. Then he stopped again. "All right, Giuseppe," he said to his model, "I'll call you again later on." The boy sprang down from the platform and immediately busied himself about the studio. Lucas had noticed nothing.

"You're in trouble, aren't you?"

Lucas made a faint movement as though he were waking out of sleep. There was something in the ring of the monk's voice that brought comfort to his soul. He had not grasped what he said; the tone of voice alone had caught his ear, and his heart opened out to him.

"You're in trouble, aren't you?" Serafio repeated.

Lucas nodded.

"Can I help you?"

Lucas shook his head.

"Is life such a burden to you, Lucas?" the gentle voice continued.

"I am not living a life," whispered Lucas with a break in his voice.

"What's the matter with you?"

"I am waiting . . ." replied Lucas as though he were talking to himself.

"What are you waiting for?"

"Waiting to be allowed to be a man again." As the words left his lips Lucas felt overcome with despair.

"But what are you now?"

"An animal!" he burst out, but immediately shrank back in terror, pressing his hand nervously to his mouth.

Serafio gazed long and anxiously at him. "Listen, Lucas," he said at last. As the young man did not answer, he added: "Will you listen to what I have to say?"

Lucas was still holding his hand to his mouth, as though to dam a flood of confidences.

"Don't you wish me to speak to you?"

"Yes, go on!" groaned the other in anguish.

"Well then, Lucas," continued the monk, "if your trouble should ever become greater than you can bear, come to me. And come to me too if your heart feels lighter. You are alone. Treat me as a brother and come to me."

The soft note of tenderness in the monk's voice soothed Lucas. "Reverend brother..." he stammered.

"No, not reverend," interrupted Serafio, "just brother... and come whenever you like."

He began to paint again.

The silence that ensued was suddenly interrupted by the sound of Cesare Bandini's voice. "Rossellino! What happened at Claudia's last night?"

Lucas pricked up his ears. The monk buried himself in his work. Rossellino went on modelling with wild violent movements. "Have you heard already?"

"Filippo was talking about it a moment ago in the garden," replied Bandini carelessly. "I happened to catch something as I passed."

"Apparently they fell out only yesterday afternoon," said Rossellino with a gruff laugh, "out there along the Arno. The Archduke was there and Claudia too. They say they came to blows over the Archduke's dog. I don't know. I wasn't there."

"But you were there in the evening, weren't you?" enquired Bandini.

Rossellino flung on the wet clay with a resounding smack. "Yes, by God! It was gorgeous! Peretti was more self-assertive than ever—you know what he is! Ercole sat as still as a statue. We were waiting for his song. But he did not sing. Then all of a sudden he called out, 'That'll do!' in a tone of command. Everybody looked at him. Peretti, who was just going to kiss Claudia, shrunk back as if he had been stung. Ercole nodded in his direction. He sat there quite calmly and nodded at him. 'Yes, I mean you, Peretti. . . . We've had enough of you. Clear out!' He spoke quite calmly. But everybody could see that he was boiling over. We were all terrified out of our wits and Claudia went pale as death."

Bandini whistled.

"Peretti went pale too," Rossellino continued. "'Are you mad?' he bawled at the Captain, or rather, he tried to bawl, but his voice gave way. 'No, I'm not mad,' said Ercole. 'I say we've had enough of you! Clear out! We've put up with you too long, you dirty beast!' That was frank enough, Bandini, frank enough in all conscience . . . and we all felt a cold shudder go down our spines. Claudia burst into loud sobs, and Peretti . . . well, the whole thing happened in a flash. Peretti seized the table and was just going to jump across it and fall upon Ercole when suddenly the Captain flung his goblet at his face and struck him square between the eyes. Peretti dropped like a felled ox, and lay stiff as a board across the table. They had to carry him away—Caligula and the others."

Again Bandini whistled. "Good!" he exclaimed. "Excellent!" And he roared with laughter. "But Ercole had better look out now," he added after a while, clicking his tongue. And he burst out into fresh roars of laughter. "Splendid! I wish I had been there to see it!"

Lucas was burning with excitement. The monk was buried in his work.

"Dirty beast!" exclaimed Bandini in high delight. "Yes, that's the word . . . that's . . ."

"Hush!" growled Rossellino. "The Captain's here!"

The glass door was gently opened, and greeting everybody with an air of complete innocence, Ercole da Moreno went over to his chair and quietly took his seat. Giuseppe immediately hurried up to him with paints, brushes and a palette.

For some minutes all was quiet. Then suddenly there was a murmur of voices all speaking at once in the garden. "Claudia's coming!" cried little Giuseppe in high glee from a corner of the studio.

Lucas closed his eyes. He could see himself on the moonlit terrace, and he felt hot all over as he had done two days previously, when Claudia had waited for him, and he had been forced to go. He did not notice that the monk at his side had left his work and vanished. All he could hear was Bandini calling out in delight, "I wonder whether Peretti is with her today. What do you think, Ercole?"

The Captain made no reply.

But for Caligula, the mulatto, who remained outside the door, Claudia was alone. She was wearing a dark dress and a subdued colored cloak, and her expression as she advanced toward Bandini was quiet and timid.

"Let me stay here a little while," she begged. "I want to be near you . . . today. . . ."

Her eyes fell on Lucas, who gazed up beseechingly at her. But she only drew herself up proudly and her sweet face hardened into an expression of angry contempt. Turning haughtily round she wandered slowly in and out among the statues, easels and furniture. By a roundabout course she at length, and apparently quite by chance, reached the Captain's armchair.

"My friend," she whispered, stopping behind it, "my friend. . . . He'll never come to me again. . . . He ought never to have been allowed to come at all. . . . This morning I sent him word that he was never to let his face be seen in my house again. Do you hear . . . my friend?"

Leaning back, the Captain looked up at Claudia and smiled. She glided up to him and kissed him on his ruddy brow just where his thick tuft of snow-white hair shot up. Then she quickly left his side.

Stopping at the door, she turned her head to Lucas, her eyes flashing. "As for you, sir," she exclaimed haughtily, "I want a word with you."

Lucas sprang up and followed her with leaden feet.

All he heard as he left the studio was a short whistle from Bandini.

Claudia crossed the courtyard and went into the garden without looking round. Lucas followed. They passed by the others. Filippo Volta looked up from his work to gaze across at them. The mulatto, Caligula, followed slowly some distance behind.

When they were under the thick overhanging foliage of the pergola, Claudia turned round so suddenly that Lucas almost fell into her arms as he staggered forward.

"You!" she cried in shrill tones, panting audibly. Her burning face was quite close to his. "You! So you spurned me, did you?"

Lucas could read the uncertainty beneath her threatening tone. It was not her anger that upset him, but this painful uncertainty which, despite her efforts to conceal it lurked in her eyes and the corners of her mouth.

Dropping on his knees, he buried his head in her dress and sobbed aloud, his despair making him oblivious of all else.

Claudia bent over him aghast.

"Hush, for heaven's sake!" she murmured in frightened tones, putting her hand over his mouth. "Child! . . . Hush!"

Lucas pulled himself together, but his shoulders and back were still heaving. She raised him to his feet. "Now tell me!" she said, speaking more gently, though she was still puzzled and astonished. "I waited for you—why did you not come?"

"I can't tell you," he replied, gazing at her, his features distorted with woe. "I really cannot." He was beside himself and his whisper sounded like a shriek of agony. "I really cannot tell you . . . but I am dying of love for you!"

She clasped him to her bosom. He could feel her kiss on his lips, and holding her close in his arms he forgot all else.

"When will you come?" she asked.

He kissed her shoulders and her neck. "Today," he whispered between the kisses, "Today!" She struggled to release herself and afraid that the movement meant a refusal, he held her fast. "Today—today!" he implored.

Gently Claudia freed herself from his embrace. "No, not today," she said, smiling graciously at him. "It cannot be today . . . but tomorrow."

"Tomorrow?" And the light went out from his eyes.

She tried to comfort him. "Well then . . . the day after tomorrow . . ." and she gazed at him in astonishment. . . . "Either the day after tomorrow or at any rate soon. Goodbye." And opening the little gate in the garden wall, she slipped out into the street.

Lucas remained rooted to the spot for some time. Caligula, the mulatto, passed him and squinting searchingly at him, slipped out through the little gate. But Lucas did not notice him.

That night the whole party was assembled in the osteria where Bandini's pupils had a private apartment of their own in which they could drink and enjoy themselves. Lucas paced restlessly up and down the stuffy old room. He found it impossible to remain seated. The fragrance of Claudia's golden hair was still about him, and his senses were still alive to the pulsating presence of her body. He was glad he could spend this evening with the others. He felt more at home with them now than he had done hitherto and more closely bound to them in heart and soul. Their presence blunted the exquisite sharpness of his joy, forcing him to moderate his spirits' wild exuberance.

Nevertheless it was impossible for him to sit still. He wandered round the table, almost dancing as he moved, making his way along the wall. The clatter of goblets and the twanging of a lute, mingled with the rise and fall of desultory conversation, fell pleasantly on his ear. He heard the sound of familiar voices, but the words they uttered sank unheeded into his being, swallowed up in the agitated flood of his thoughts, as drops of rain are swallowed up in the sea.

His restless eyes gazed round the walls, from which a strange array of figures, heads and arabesques seemed to beckon to him. There were saints and courtesans, kings and fools, mountains, churches and Palaces, all jumbled together. Licentious love scenes were depicted, while the heads of well-known men and women, often bewilderingly lifelike, looked down on him as though they were about to speak, only to become mere caricatures again on the whitewashed walls. Everything was there that the wanton spirits of young artists, in the fullness of youth and vigor and under the inspiration of unbridled fancy, could splash on to the wall. Lucas feasted his eyes on the mute tumult of color and charcoal, delighting in the consummate harmony achieved by the endless medley of forms, picking out with all the extravagant joy of recognition the writing that was familiar to him, and noting other kinds that were strange and probably belonged to days long since gone by. With his hand in his pocket, he was turning a piece of charcoal about in his fingers, stimulated by the multifarious forms he saw before him, but shyness prevented him from going any further. He did not feel sufficiently advanced to dare set any product of his meager talent beside the daring achievements of the others.

All he felt he wanted to do was to wander round and round the table. Then suddenly he overheard a remark:

"The Archduke will not wait. He is going home . . . he won't wait until Bandini's picture is finished!"

He stood rooted to the spot and listened. It was Filippo Volta who had just spoken.

"Bandini will finish it in a fortnight . . . he won't take a day longer," replied Rossellino sullenly.

Filippo Volta laughed good-naturedly. "And I tell you the Prince is going off in three or four days' time . . . not a moment later!"

Lucas clapped his hands together and listened nay, his whole soul expanded and laid itself bare as though it were harkening to the strains of the sweetest music.

Presently Cosimo Rubinardo came along and joined in the conversation. He spoke with modest dignity, as he had done in the old days when he was a rich man and used to shower down ducats on the artists with a liberal hand. He seemed to regard his poverty with indifference, and even with a touch of pride.

"It's quite true, Pietro," he said, leaning toward Rossellino, "the Archduke is not going to stop here more than three or four days now. They were discussing the subject this morning at Claudia's."

Lucas's heart leaped with the joy and confidence that flooded his being, making his chest heave, loosening the choking he had felt in his throat for weeks, so that he could have shouted for joy. He almost capered round the room on his toes—three, four days; they might be five for all he cared! His thoughts shouted one against the other in his brain, until his ears buzzed. Three, four days—and then freedom! Freedom! Then I shall be here in Florence; here, or in Rome, but at all events where I choose to be. Oh how easy it has all been! How foolish of me to have been so miserable! What have I suffered after all? Suffered? Why it was nothing! A joke—a dream—three or four days . . . and then I shall be like other men!

"No, he's not going back to Vienna," he heard the Captain's rich, sonorous voice saying. "He's going to travel about the Empire—going to Worms, I believe, or perhaps to Augsburg."

Lucas went up to the table and dropped into his seat.

"What's all this about Worms?" he asked with a laugh.

The Captain turned his merry eyes toward him.

"What's all this about Worms?" Lucas repeated scornfully. "Worms!... Florence is better!" he added, accentuating his words so as to make them sound comical.

"In a fortnight Bandini will have finished the picture," repeated Rossellino stubbornly.

"Then I can look forward to the feast," said Ercole da Moreno contentedly.

"What feast?" cried Lucas at the top of his voice.

The Captain looked down at him, cheerful though surprised.

"A magnificent feast, my son," he explained, and under his white mustache he seemed to be smacking his lips in luxurious anticipation. "Bandini always gives a feast when he has finished a picture. His house is open from one morning to the next, authors come and make speeches or recite impromptu verses. All kinds of mountebanks come in; in fact the whole town is there. Anyone who likes can drink a glass of wine and go in and have a look at Bandini's picture. But he himself sits down to table with us from one morning to the next, and we have him all to ourselves. I'm delighted!"

Lucas brought his fist down on the table. "Quite right! I'm delighted too!" And he crowed for joy. "I'm delighted too!" Everyone laughed.

Suddenly a thin man in a black coat slipped into the room. The fact that he was very lame was hardly noticeable for he did not walk, but hopped, skipped and jumped about continuously. His face was very thin and so yellow that he might just have been recovering from the jaundice. His head was covered with thick iron-gray hair, springing from a low forehead; his black eyes shone feverishly and he held his toothless mouth ecstatically open.

"Here she is!" he cried in a half-audible whisper. "I'll bring her to you!" and he pointed convulsively to a little girl who was standing at the door. "Allow me to introduce you to the little marchioness, the Principessa Leonora . . . there she stands before the galaxy of illustrious artists and her magnificent young life is about to begin." He spoke very fast, as though he were reading, and so low that he might almost have been talking to himself. "Come in, Leonora! Come in, Principessa!"

The child stepped innocently up to the table. She might have been twelve or thirteen years of age, and the youthful contours of her gracefully molded little body were outlined under her flimsy frock. Her pale face was extraordinarily noble, and full of a mysterious pride. She turned her beautiful eyes gravely from one to the other.

The thin man continued to jump and skip about. "First inspect her, inspect her carefully . . . and the artist among you, the master among you, the man who has eyes will be able to see at once. . . . The man who cannot see that she is an aristocrat, Leonora, a Principessa, will perhaps remember that Zacco Zaccone never descends to common prostitutes. He will perhaps remember that Zacco Zaccone can recognize Aphrodite's favorites when they are still in their cots, nay, even before they have quickened in the womb. Don't forget that Zacco Zaccone brought up Superba, whom the King of Naples made his slave; that he discovered Vittoria, who is sought after in Rome by cardinals, cardinals' favorites and German princes, and that he presented you with Claudia, who is now sparkling in Florence like a diamond! Come, Principessa Leonora!" he cried, and putting to his chin a little violin which he had been flourishing in his hand, he began to play.

Rossellino and Filippo Volta moved the table aside, and Lucas, making room, went and sat close to the Captain.

The rich tone of the little violin was almost like a human voice. Zacco Zaccone played a solemn melody, and in the space previously occupied by the table, the girl began to dance, slowly, with stirring grace, her proud pale face uplifted.

Suddenly Zacco Zaccone stopped and, darting toward the girl and prancing round her, undressed her with a few lightning touches. "She can be painted . . . and she can be modelled in bronze and in silver," he said as he did so, while the white young body gradually emerged from the clothes. "In silver or in ivory . . . she is in fact ivory herself . . . Eleanora . . . she can be painted as a saint or as an angel of God . . . as a young nymph. . . ." He stopped for a moment, and pointed at the girl's firm little breasts. . . . "She would do equally well for Psyche or for Artemis . . . you can paint her and you can love her," he continued, squatting on the floor and pulling the child's clothes away from under her feet. She stood calm and naked before the men. "You can love her as she is, and intoxicate yourselves with her, for she is so full of fire that my fingers burn when I touch her. . . ."

And getting up, he seized the violin. "Come, Leonora . . . she will be just what Superba was . . . she will be as great as Vittoria . . . and she will be what Claudia is . . . from this day onward! Today her young life, blessed by all the gods, begins . . . !" The sound of the violin drowned his voice, but he seemed to be muttering to himself as he played.

Leonora danced. The men, sitting in a semi-circle round her, looked on in silence as they drank.

She danced in slow, smooth, rhythmic movements, as though she were playing and yet serious as thought. Her frail body, which looked as though it had but then been created, twisting and turning, bending and sway-ing, with graceful pride, seemed, like her close shut lips, to know more than her eyes. Her eyes, as they gazed calmly in front of her, seemed to know more than her soul, and the mild radiance of her soul suffused her sweet childish features.

"Magnificent!" muttered Rossellino hoarsely, leaning toward the Captain.

"Yes . . . she must have been very beautiful once," Lucas heard Ercole da Moreno reply calmly.

He glanced in astonishment at the Captain. "What does he mean?" he whispered, turning to Filippo Volta.

Filippo smiled courteously. "Oh . . . that's Ercole's way. . . . Didn't you know?"

Zacco Zaccone was helping little Leonora to dress. "We shall come back again," he said, still tripping about. "We shall come back! . . . We shall be sent for . . . you will dream about us . . . you will long for us. . . ."

"In a fortnight's time Bandini's picture will be finished," interrupted Filippo Volta, "and then we shall have a feast."

Zacco Zaccone gave a tittering laugh. "In a fortnight's time we shall long have been famous . . . in a fortnight's time we shall be as flooded with light as the earth is two minutes before dawn ... but we shall come ... your feast would not be a feast if we were not there. ..."

So saying, he went off with the girl, who left the room without vouchsafing a glance to anyone.

Rossellino and Volta pushed the table back into its place, and they all drank again.

"I shall make a statuette of her," said Rossellino to himself. His face was flushed and he held his head thrown back thoughtfully between his shoulders. "A silver statuette."

Whereupon the Captain began to sing, sitting erect in his chair, with one hand on his goblet, and his white hair flaming high above his fine brow. His voice seemed to flood the room with light.

> "Pray let me live right long, O Lord!
> Pray leave me here below!
> And show me love and grace, O Lord!
> For dead men cannot pray, O Lord,

But only they can praise Thee, Lord,
Who stay down here below!"

The others leaned back in their chairs, looking up at the ceiling, as though they were following the song with their eyes, as it hovered above their heads. Right reverently they listened, and their souls were filled with joy by the wondrous rhythm of that song. Lucas took a deep breath. "In three, four days!" he thought.

Presently they got up to go.

Outside the square lay bathed in the light of the full moon. They were walking close together round the Captain, when suddenly, from the dark shadow of a wall, three men dashed out. They seemed to be a band of drunken revellers, too intoxicated to move out of the way of the group of artists. But everything that followed happened so quickly that no one could tell what really took place, and it was only when they found themselves being violently hustled that Lucas and his companions discovered that the men were masked. Their hands immediately flew to their swords and daggers. But the next moment the Captain, with a stifled groan, dropped heavily to the ground, and the three men vanished like lightning into the blackness of a little alley. In the twinkling of an eye they had completely disappeared and not even the echo of their footsteps could be heard.

Ercole da Moreno was lying with his face on the white, moonlit cobblestones.

Lucas, like his companions, stood speechless staring down at him. He saw his arms move in a strange uncontrolled way, and his legs twitch, and with feelings of horror he was suddenly reminded of the last spasmodic movements of a slaughtered animal. They turned the poor man over, and found that he was already lying in a pool of blood that had collected under his chest, and that his face was covered with the blood that was pouring from his mouth.

The others shouted and raised a clamor. Cosimo Rubinardo burst into loud sobs. "This is Peretti's doing!" bellowed Rossellino, mad with rage.

Lucas stared down at the dead man. With his ghastly white, blood-stained face and dim eyes staring up at the moon, he certainly bore a remote resemblance to the beloved friend of a moment ago, and yet he had suddenly become so strange that Lucas felt as though be were looking on him for the first time.

The dog was creeping restlessly about the courtyard of the Palace. There were signs of activity everywhere—in the stables and on the stairs. It was early morning but servants were running hither and thither, shouting to one another. The grooms were polishing the harness and the trappings, and the dog, who had searched all the rooms, had not succeeded in finding his master anywhere.

Count Waltersburg had laughed when the dog entered his room, and had driven him out again. Master Pointner, who came across him in the vestibule, kicked him as he bounded up to him with a look of enquiry in his eyes.

Cambyses then proceeded to skulk about the courtyard, not knowing what to do. He ran into the garden, whining to himself and bounded along the passage and up the steps, sniffing as he went. At last he went back to the stables.

Here Caspar, the young groom, caught sight of him and looked at him for a moment laughing. "Well, Cambyses," he said at last, "looking for your master, eh?"

The dog went up to him wagging his tail.

"You must wait a bit," said Caspar, bending over him and patting him. "Yes, my friend . . . today your master is doing exactly what you are always doing, . . . He's away! Yes, yes, the master has gone away to enjoy himself, just as Cambyses does . . . he has a sweetheart and has been spending the night with her. Yes, just look at me, Cambyses. Do you imagine that only dogs do that sort of thing? Oh no, my friend, we men have hearts as well as you." And Caspar laughed.

Suddenly the dog pricked up his ears and capered and bounded round the courtyard. Along the passage, from the direction of the street, heavy footsteps could be heard marching in step. A closely curtained sedan chair was being carried in, but the dog knew at once that his master was in it.

The sedan chair was set down at the foot of the steps and the Archduke alighted. The dog followed him and lay at his feet on the floor while breakfast was served. The Archduke breakfasted alone, eating quickly as though he were very hungry. Presently Master Pointner came in. He cleared his throat and remained standing at the door.

"Well, what is it, Pointner?"

"His Imperial Highness might perhaps like to come up to the room just overhead. . . ."

"Why? I'm tired. I would like to have a couple of hours' sleep."

"Well, I mean just look in as you pass—just for fun."

The Archduke rose from the table. Pointner showed the way.

"There's a cat up there in the marble hall," he explained. "I have had all the chairs taken out and the doors closed. But one door has a grill, so we can see everything."

"See what?"

"Why, Cambyses chasing the cat. She can't possibly get away. He'll chase her and break her neck."

"Cats! Fetch 'em! Where are they?" exclaimed the Archduke, turning to Cambyses.

They had reached the door with the grill and Pointner pushed the dog in. "Fetch 'em!" he shouted.

In the empty, gleaming white, marble hall, a tabby cat was creeping along the wall. When the dog sprang in, she stood still, arching her back and hissing and spitting.

"Catch her! Fetch her!" cried the two voices from the door.

The dog ran forward; the cat swept along in front of him, retreating in orderly fashion, quickly glancing round for some means of escape or a ledge upon which to take refuge. But the smooth marble walls offered no hope. At last with one spring she succeeded in getting on to a window-ledge. When the dog, rushing forward, came to a standstill in front of her, she hissed at him, and taking advantage of a moment's hesitation on his part, she jumped across him into the middle of the hall. Whereupon the dog chased her round and round, bowled her over, making her roll up like a ball, circled round her and gave her time to assume the defensive once more, when he again advanced toward her wagging his tail, as though he were trying to persuade her to give him another run.

"He's not doing anything to her! See, he's only playing with her," cried the Archduke.

"Wretched brute!" exclaimed Pointner indignantly. "Catch her, catch her!"

And he continued shouting and roaring until, excited by the noise, the dog charged again, and drove the cat round and round. No matter how near he got to her, however, he never snapped at her, but held his head up high, as though pity or disgust prevented him from touching her.

"Will you catch her—catch her, you rascal! Wait a minute, I'll show you!" roared Pointner.

Suddenly the cat turned round, and standing up to the astonished dog, arched her back and scratched him so fiercely across the face that he retreated howling and ran away with his nose to the floor.

"Enough!" he heard the Archduke say. At the same time he caught the sound of the door-handle being turned and the door was slightly opened. Making a dash for the narrow aperture, he pressed himself into it so as to open it wider, and darted out between Master Pointner's legs, making him stagger to one side.

The Archduke pointed to the drops of blood on the floor, which left a red trail behind the dog as he dashed through the vestibule of the hall and down the stairs. "He's bleeding!"

"Let him bleed!" muttered Pointner.

The studio was empty when Lucas entered it. Only Bandini was standing before his easel and though as a rule he never looked up from his work, he now started back in surprise.

"Do you know what has happened?" he asked Lucas.

But Lucas had been snatched away from human society on the previous day, and had only been himself since midnight. He knew nothing.

Flinging down his palette, Bandini began to pace restlessly up and down the room between the easels and the furniture, constantly putting his hand to his brow as though his head were aching.

"So they left their mark on you too?" he observed

slowly, coming up to Lucas. Lucas looked up in astonishment as Bandini pointed to the angry scratch running across his brow to his eyebrow. Lucas turned pale.

"No...." he stammered, putting his hand quickly to
the freshly cicatrized wound, "... that didn't happen ...
on that occasion."

Without taking any further notice of him, Bandini
turned away and began pacing up and down again,
stopping short and then moving on once more.

"They are looking for him ..." he said. "They are
looking for him everywhere ... they won't give up until
they catch him ... they won't let him rest until ... until
they find him...."

Lucas was ashamed to ask whom he meant.

Suddenly Bandini stopped still and glanced all
round the studio. "God knows where he can be," he
exclaimed angrily. "The scoundrel has taken good care
to hide himself."

Little by little Lucas put two and two together and
discovered what Bandini was talking about. Peretti had
vanished. His Palace was locked up, his servants had fled

with their master, and no one except the porter had been left behind. The suspicion that everybody had formed was now confirmed. Ercole had been murdered by a band of ruffians hired by Peretti, for whom a continuous search had been made since the previous day. Filippo Volta was looking for him high and low, as were also Pietro Rossellino, Cosimo Rubinardo and many others.

The studios of all the painters, sculptors and goldsmiths in Florence had been deserted ever since the previous morning, their inmates being engaged in hunting for Peretti. They hoped to seize him and if possible kill him then and there, or else stalk him down and keep a sharp eye on him, not letting him out of sight until help arrived and he and his companions could be overpowered. They were scouring the country in all directions on horseback, hunting for him through woods and valleys, questioning the peasants, peeping through keyholes and spying in monasteries, while a certain number of them remained in Florence keeping watch on the Palaces which were known to belong to his friends.

Bandini continued to pace restlessly up and down

the studio. Presently he stopped in front of Ercole's capacious armchair and stood lost in thought before the charming little Madonna on the easel. At last he passed his hand caressingly over the velvet back of the chair, and shaking his head, moved away.

"This evening they will be back," he said.

"Why?" enquired Lucas.

"They'll have to be back when we bury him, of course." His words sounded like a reproof.

"When?" asked Lucas timidly. "Where will he be buried?"

"Don't you know?" exclaimed Bandini, with a look of surprise. "Why, up in Fiesole, in the cathedral."

"Oh yes, of course," exclaimed Lucas, as if the fact had momentarily slipped his memory. But the words, uttered under his breath, were inaudible.

Bandini went back to his easel and began to paint, perfunctorily, absent-mindedly. Presently he laid his palette and brushes down again, and going over to Ercole's place, sat down in the armchair, where he remained silently seated for some time.

Lucas too remained still and motionless and, with his hands in his lap, stared into space. Everything that had happened rushed in a sad, confused medley through his brain.

"Oh!" exclaimed Bandini suddenly, as though he had forgotten something. The cry brought Lucas back to earth. "Oh!" cried Bandini, rising from Ercole's armchair and clapping his hand to his brow. And going over to one of the tall carved cabinets, he unlocked it and took out a little picture. Lucas saw the gleam of the gilt frame.

"Come here, my son."

Lucas hurried over to Bandini's side. He was holding the little picture in his hands. "This must be taken to the Archduke at the Palace. But I don't want to go there myself today. I don't want to," he repeated with impatient emphasis. "I don't want to talk to anyone today!" Then growing calmer, he added. "But I promised to let the Archduke have this now, and I don't want him to have to wait for it. He is off in three days."

Lucas quivered with joy. He had heard it again and this time it was certain—in three days!

"You go," Bandini continued, "and give the picture to the Archduke or to Count Waltersburg, or someone. Tell them that I am not well—you understand!"

Lucas took the picture from his hands and started back in astonishment. It was Claudia's portrait, touched in with light rapid strokes in beautiful transparent colors, and so lifelike that she looked as though she might be listening to every word they were saying.

The shadow of a fleeting smile hovered round Bandini's lips as Lucas stood in absorbed enraptured contemplation of the picture.

"Just put a cloth round it," he said kindly, "and be off!"

In the broad echoing corridor of the Palace, Lucas could not resist the temptation of going up to the open door and looking out into the courtyard which lay dazzling white in the sunshine before him. Across it the stable doors stood open, and the grooms were chattering together amid the stamping and snorting of the horses.

Lucas turned round and ascending the stairs, crossed two rooms and went through doors, apartments and corridors, all of which were quite familiar to him. He noticed that the servants were everywhere busy packing trunks, and preparing for the Archduke's departure. He was directed to Ugolino Corsini, whom he found at a table covered with books. Ugolino took the picture, gazed at it spellbound, and, turning his chubby face to Lucas, listened in silence while the latter explained that Bandini was indisposed and was unable to wait upon His Imperial Highness in person.

Lucas then took his leave and, as he wandered back aimlessly through the rooms, not paying any attention to where he was going, he suddenly found himself in the large empty hall, where, on the previous day, he had been made to chase the cat. He was seized with violent uneasiness. His eye fell on the door with the grill at the other end of the hall, and he ran toward it, filled with a sudden fear of seeing two familiar figures behind it, shouting wild commands at his head. Unconsciously he clasped a hand to his brow, touched the scar above his eye, which all at once had begun to sting, and then tore open the door in order to escape.

As he reached the outer vestibule, he suddenly found Master Pointner, who was just about to enter, standing in front of him. Seized with uncontrollable rage, he raised his fist without saying a word, and struck Master Pointner a violent blow in the face. Then he dashed past him as Pointner staggered to the wall, caught a glimpse, as he sprang toward the stairs, of the nose in his fat face bleeding, and was at the foot of the stairs before his victim could even cry out.

As he went out at the gate, his body swayed, his feet tripped lightly; in his clenched fist he tried to hold like a prize the blow he had just given. He laughed, gave a sigh of relief, laughed again.

Coming to a standstill on the bridge, he gazed with joyful eyes upon the city, which, cut in two at this spot by the river, lay spread out to view before his eyes, and once more he had the intoxicated feeling that the whole of life belonged to him. Wondering where to spend his time until evening, he started as a daring thought flashed through his mind, and quickly ran on.

At the door of Claudia's house he knocked loudly,

afraid that delay might sap his courage. Caligula, the mulatto, opened the door, squinted at him in astonishment, and looked as though he meant to refuse him admittance. But Lucas pushed past him, and, catching sight of Peppina, called out to her. She tripped up to him with her usual mincing steps, smiled as though she knew all, and led him through a long corridor into the garden. Caligula gazed malevolently after them.

When Claudia's dark blue sparkling eyes rested enquiringly on him, searching his face, Lucas again lost confidence. The ecstasy with which Claudia's presence always filled him became more violent than ever. His presence of mind and composure failed him, and in trying to pull himself together, he exhausted himself in an effort at least to master his speech.

"So you come when you choose?" said Claudia. Astonishment and curiosity lay hid behind the haughty tone she adopted to conceal them.

"I come . . . I come . . ." stammered Lucas ". . . when I am allowed to."

Side by side they walked on the fine, golden gravel

of the narrow garden paths. Against a background of yew, which shielded them from the eyes of the world, the magnolias on their bare stems nodded their great blooms at them. The pines spread their peaceful branches silently above their heads, and at their feet the lawn was studded with beds of glowing hyacinths.

"Everybody has gone," said Claudia, "they are all looking for that blackguard Peretti! If only they could find him! I wish he were dead! . . . I wish I had got Caligula to strangle him . . . or I wish," she added in calm bitter tones, "Ercole da Moreno had killed him that night at table."

Presently she turned her face to Lucas. "But it's not right for all of them to go away, and for no one to remember me. Not one of them has been near me, either yesterday or today. Even Cosimo has left me . . . you alone have come." And again she smiled at him.

Lucas raised his arms, but she paid no heed to the gesture. "Oh my own Ercole!" she exclaimed mournfully, "My poor Ercole . . . my friend! . . . My friend!" And she bowed her head. "My friend!" she repeated in a whisper.

"Claudia . . ." said Lucas softly.

"Yes . . . you . . ." she replied gazing at him. "You are here, but not because of Ercole. What do you know of Ercole? Why have you come . . . why today? Why precisely now?"

"I love you . . ." he began, but his voice failed him and he stopped.

Claudia nodded. "You love me . . ." she said, nodding gently again and again, "you love me. . . ."

As he stood desperate before her, she suddenly seized him by the shoulder. . . . "And you have made me wait for you . . . you scorned me . . . you made me wait the whole night."

Lucas bowed his head. "No one knows what I have suffered," he gasped, pale as death, wringing his hands and scarcely able to breathe. "No one has any idea what I am suffering. . . . If I were as rich as the others. . . ."

"Hush!" cried Claudia gently. "If you were rich, you could never be as pale as you are now; there would never be a look of such devotion in your face, or such longing in your eyes."

And she put her arms about his neck and kissed him.

They went indoors. Crossing the terrace from which Lucas had stolen away in despair on that moonlight night, they entered the room from which he had fled.

It was late at night when Lucas left Claudia's house, and hurried through the streets and out at the gate leading on to the road to Fiesole. As soon as he was out of the town he walked quickly, passing by other men whom in the dim light of the waning moon he could not recognize. Before he reached Badia he was overtaken by two horsemen, who shouted to him. They were Filippo Volta and Rossellino. "Jump up!" cried Filippo. Lucas sprang up behind him and thus they rode up to Fiesole.

In the middle of the cathedral which was illumined right up to the vaulted roof by candles and torches, and filled with the monotonous chants of the Franciscan friars, the black draped structure of the catafalque rose aloft, so that only the slanting sides of the coffin containing the last earthly remains of the Captain could be seen. But, at the head, Ercole's snow-white shock of hair was visible above the shell. Lucas was suddenly over-come with violent grief as, on looking up, his eyes fell upon those still, white locks.

Bandini had just entered, while Rossellino and a number of other young men, whom Lucas either did not know; or whom he had only met quite casually—artists and old army officers—had also arrived. They nodded to one another, stepped forward, formed a circle round the catafalque, and stood still and solemn in their places. Overcome with emotion, some of them were biting their lips and others breathing loud and heavily.

Behind them, in the pews on either side, Franciscan friars were kneeling, chanting their litany. The strains echoed harsh and tragic through the stone arches of the church.

Lucas took his place among his comrades, gazing up at the catafalque with his eyes fixed on the spot where the white shock of hair rose above the edge of the cof-fin like frozen flames.

Suddenly a tremor passed through the circle of mourners. They all seized their swords, and with one

simultaneous movement, planted them point downward in front of them, and crossed their hands on their
hats over the pommels. Whereupon Bandini's voice was
heard:

"Pray let me live right long, O Lord!"

They all joined in.

The song rose above the litany of the friars, which
instantly ceased. Spreading far and wide, the noble joy
of the song soared aloft, enveloping in its vital rhythm
the friend who had passed away.

And Lucas saw a tremor pass through the shock of
snow-white hair above the coffin.

When Lucas entered the studio, he found Count
Waltersburg talking to Bandini. "Tomorrow is our last
day here," he was saying. "We set off on our journey the
day after tomorrow, just before midday. Can't you finish the picture by tomorrow?"

Clutching the back of his chair, Lucas looked across
at the couple. Bandini shrugged his shoulders. "It will
take me at least two or three weeks longer."

Waltersburg tapped the floor impatiently with the point of his shoe.

"That's annoying—most annoying!"

"Besides, I don't feel in the mood to work at all," continued Bandini slowly. "This business of the Captain—you know what I mean, my lord—is still lying heavy on my heart."

"It's the devil!" cried Waltersburg. "What a curious crowd you have in this country! Why, a fellow has just given our Imperial master's Groom-of-the-Chamber a blow in the face. . . . Think of it, in broad daylight, and in the Palace too. Happened only two days ago."

"Yes," replied Bandini with a smile, "the people here need understanding, they soon flare up."

"I beg your pardon," said Waltersburg courteously, still looking astonished, "Pointner had never in his life set eyes on the fellow or exchanged a word with him. According to Pointner, the man glared at him mad with rage, and then, without a word, punched him violently in the face!"

"And the man himself . . . what happened to him?" enquired Bandini.

"Nothing!" cried Waltersburg, his voice shriller than ever. "He vanished as though the ground had swallowed him up. It was altogether a most unfortunate business for Pointner. A real piece of bad luck. He's lying seriously ill now and Heaven knows when he'll be on his legs again."

"Was it such a terrific blow then?"

"No, not at all," replied Waltersburg, pity, good-nature and astonishment mingling in his voice. "The blow itself didn't hurt him much. As far as that is concerned, he is practically well again. But the fright was a great shock, his liver is upset and he is suffering from cold shivers."

"Fright?" observed Bandini with a smile. "Fright in addition to all the rest?"

"That's just it," said Waltersburg, shrugging his shoulders hopelessly, "Pointner thinks the affair with that fellow is only just a beginning. He imagines that he has secret enemies here who are determined to take his life. He is confined to bed and shivers so that his teeth chatter. It seems almost impossible that a man in his prime like Pointner could have become such a complete wreck in a single night. The doctors hold out little hope. He is completely broken up."

Lucas slunk away. Going out by the little back door through which the monk always vanished when Claudia appeared, he slipped silent as a shadow into the garden and stole out into the street where he wandered aimlessly about. It was impossible for him to work that day; he could not remain in the studio. He felt too restless. Only for an instant did his unrepentant thoughts revert to Pointner, lying ill in bed. But, with a snap of his fingers he dismissed all recollection of him from his mind as perfectly futile.

"Tomorrow once again," he muttered to himself as he went along. "Tomorrow I shall once again have to undergo the transformation—once more for the last time, and then I shall be free!" Nevertheless he was not overwhelmed with joy at the thought; he had a feeling of uneasiness that increased every moment and became so insistent that he grew quite nervous.

Slackening his pace, he meditated returning to

the studio. His mood inclined him to seek the company of his fellows, for he found solitude intolerable. Nevertheless he shunned the studio; it could not help him that day. The empty armchair in front of the little Madonna picture would only serve to remind him of the Captain's death, while the deserted seats of his fellow-students would proclaim that they were still hunting for the murderer. He also felt unfit for work. That day was too close to the decisive hour of his life, it was too full of impatient expectation, to make it possible for him to work. Nor did he look for any comfort in Bandini's presence. He longed for someone in whom to confide. Yet he stood in too great awe of Bandini to turn to him.

All unconsciously he found himself in front of Claudia's house. Caligula, the mulatto, opened the door to him. His thick pouting lips smiled broadly as he announced that his mistress was away.

"Where?" exclaimed Lucas, overcome with disappointment.

"She didn't tell me where," replied Caligula, his great fat body shaking with laughter.

Lucas made another attempt to push past him; but Caligula seized him by the shoulder and Lucas could feel the iron grip of his soft fingers, the cold clamminess of which penetrated through his coat to his skin. But at the same moment he felt convinced that Caligula had spoken the truth, and that the house was empty. Nevertheless he raised a threatening fist:

"Take your hand off, you scoundrel, or I'll . . ."

Pulling a face and blinking as though the blow had already fallen, Caligula set him free, and Lucas walked down the corridor, calling for Peppina. She came up, her sphinx-like smile seeming to say she could not tell all she knew. She gave him the news. Claudia had gone to Poggio a Caiano with the Austrian Prince and his suite. They were to have a banquet there. Yes, he had guessed aright, the banquet was to be held in the country Palace which stood empty most of the year. She would probably not return until late at night or on the following day.

Meanwhile they had reached the garden. The mulatto had followed them some distance behind. Lucas went up on to the little terrace; the door leading to Claudia's room stood open. He stood on the black and white tiles, between the two flaming azaleas in their stone vases, oblivious of Peppina who, with a provocative smile, remained at his side, and unmindful of the mulatto who was watching him from behind the yew hedge. He gazed round the garden and peeped into Claudia's room; but everything looked deserted and meaningless, like the wings of a theatre when the play is over.

The sky had become overcast and the day was gray and gloomy. He was seized with acute qualms which fell upon him like heavy veils oppressing his soul. He felt he must speak to somebody, that he would die if he remained alone. Silently he crept away from Claudia's house.

Through the noisy bustling streets he wandered, enveloped in his qualms and his melancholy, oblivious to the magic and stir of the life about him. His longing to speak to a fellow creature made him hasten his steps, yet his feet felt leaden. As he crossed the great square in front of the monastery of San Marco, he thought of the Captain who had been struck his death-blow there and fallen on those very stones. But it all seemed unreal to him now, buried in the long distant past. He was surprised to find how little the recollection moved him. Nevertheless he was aware that somewhere deep down in his innermost being there was pain and mourning for Ercole, though the anxieties of that day had buried them out of sight.

At the gate of the monastery he pulled eagerly at the bell, and when the door was opened he asked excitedly to be allowed to speak to Brother Serafio.

He had to wait, but at last Serafio arrived and led him to his cell, a tiny little room, the cramped space in which brought them into close proximity, while the unspotted surface of its whitewashed walls seemed to make it impossible to conceal a single thought. Going over to his desk which was in the window and was covered with books, parchments and documents, he pointed to the bed and invited Lucas to be seated.

Lucas sat down and said nothing. The monk turned over the pages of a book. For a long while the room was buried in silence.

"Do you want me to do anything?" Serafio asked after a time in low, compassionate tones.

Lucas started. "Must I go?" he asked.

But Serafio made a sign to him. "No, stay here!" he replied.

For a few moments they sat in silence. At last Serafio said: "Will you pray with me?"

Lucas passed his hand through his hair and glanced about him. "If you wish me to, reverend Brother . . . but I don't know. I don't believe I can pray now. . . ."

"I do not wish it," replied the monk. "Nobody can wish you to pray. One should pray just as one eats and drinks. It ought to be like sleep. . . ." He hesitated. . . . "Or like waking up."

"Wait until you feel the influence of the peace that reigns here," he added after a while.

"Here?" cried Lucas.

"Don't you agree with me?" asked the monk, gazing at him.

Lucas shook his head vigorously. "No! It is only quiet here. If I were here alone . . . no . . . I would rather be in my grave!" He put his hand to his throat. "One is so far away from things here—cut off from everything—imprisoned!"

"Oh, if that is the case . . ." said Serafio with a smile.

"I am waiting," said Lucas, as though he were talking to himself, his fists tight clenched on his knees. "I am waiting . . . I am waiting! . . . but the time goes by so slowly!"

"Brother," observed the monk, "there are coals of fire in your soul . . . and they are burning too fiercely . . . I have been watching you for a long while, and I pity you. . . ."

Lucas lowered his eyes.

"You love your work," continued the monk. "As you sit by my side at Bandini's you work fast and feverishly. And then the next moment you disappear, quite regularly. One day you are there and the next you are gone. Do you go and seek life elsewhere than in the place God has allotted to you?"

Lucas looked up eagerly. He longed to open his heart and tell everything. But a sudden fit of fear sealed his lips. What if he were accused of associating with women of low repute . . . ? He turned the matter over in his mind. Tomorrow, tomorrow, for the last time, he would have to undergo the accursed metamorphosis again. On the following day the Archduke would leave Florence and everything would be over. In a fortnight, and certainly in a year's time, nobody would remember that he was always disappearing now. Nobody would ever know anything about it; nobody would ever hear about it. Was he going to confide his secret to the monk now, and let him share it on the last day, and thus possess it forever, for the whole of the future that lay before him? And wringing his hands in despair, he was silent.

The monk had been watching him. "Do you remember," he said, "that day in Bandini's studio, when you used those very words—'I am waiting, I am waiting'?"

"Yes," replied Lucas, nodding thoughtfully. "And I am waiting still!"

"Waiting to be allowed to be a human being . . . ?" Lucas started in fear. "That is what you said on that occasion, didn't you?" the monk continued.

"Yes, that is what I am waiting for!" cried Lucas with passionate emphasis.

"I do not know what you mean, brother," and Serafio's voice rung soft and low . . . "to be a human being. How few of us succeed in living like human beings. I pray for that end myself, I struggle to achieve it—but it is hard."

"Oh, you don't understand!" exclaimed Lucas, looking at him out of the corner of his eyes.

"Are you unhappy because you are poor?" asked Serafio with a smile.

"It's making me go to pieces!" cried Lucas.

"You will not go to pieces," replied Serafio kindly. "You are strong!"

Lucas shook his head. "Humiliation casts one to the ground, and one has to eat the dust!" he replied. "But worse still, one grows accustomed to eating dust. . . . So of what avail is my strength?"

Serafio laid a hand on his shoulder. "Be comforted, brother. Everyone abases himself some time or other, not only the poor. Everyone abases himself. Men abase themselves for Palaces, for wealth, for a woman, for a throne."

"That is different," said Lucas, shaking his head.

The monk smiled again. "Do you think so?"

"I know it," replied Lucas. "You forget that many a man who suffers humiliation for the sake of a crust of bread would not abase himself for all the treasures of the world, or for any woman either, or any throne on earth, if only he had bread."

"Maybe!" And Serafio returned to his desk and gazed in front of him with a look of astonishment in his eyes. "Maybe..." he repeated, turning over the pages of a book. "But see what stands here," and he beckoned to Lucas to come over to him.

Lucas sprang to his feet and went over to his side. Serafio had opened a manuscript yellow with age, and pointing to a passage, he read aloud: "If so be thou art poor on earth, thou must spend half thy life as a dog, that thou mayest spend the other half as a man among men."

"Who wrote that?" cried Lucas staggering back.

Serafio looked up in astonishment.

"Who wrote that?" repeated Lucas.

"A holy man, who lived two hundred years ago," replied Serafio, "the hermit of Mount Amiata. He learned wisdom and knew the way of the world ... and see how wonderfully he agrees with you."

Lucas had gone pale and his eyes were full of tears. He turned away as if to go.

But Serafio held him back. "Just one thing more—do not lose hold of your soul, brother. Be brave! You have wonderful powers within you. I saw that on the very first day. Success lies in you, and in your heart is the mirror of the world. You will triumph over all your difficulties. You will be great!" He stopped—"provided you meet with no misfortune," he added gently in conclusion. And embracing Lucas, he pressed him tenderly to his breast and let him go. "God keep you!"

Lucas ran out into the street.

He wandered about the town until the evening. The old fears had not left him. But in order to escape from their oppression he sought out those parts of the city where lively people congregated and laughter and song rang out. He followed the crowd streaming through the busy streets. He peered into the faces of the girls, watched the smartly dressed, high-spirited young noblemen strolling by, noted the passage of the gorgeous sedan chairs and coaches. He looked up to the windows of the Palaces, which, now that it was dark, were ablaze with lighted candelabra. But before long his eyes hardly noticed the scene about him and his melancholy gripped him more powerfully than ever.

"What is the matter with me?" he cried to himself. "I have only to wait until tomorrow! For the last time! Why do I tremble instead of rejoicing?" But in vain did he struggle against his fear. Like an invisible octopus with myriad arms, it closed about him, held him fast and gradually throttled him.

"God in Heaven!" he groaned, "let it be the last time!" And now he felt he wanted to pray, but his thoughts ran riot in his brain. Why did things come so easily to other people? Why were they allowed to possess life freely without any pain or discomfort? They had no idea what to do with it. They did not regard it as a gift, they took it as their due. Meanwhile he had nothing . . . he was an outcast. Why?

Suddenly he thought of Captain Ercole da Moreno and was overcome with excruciating grief. He saw him before his mind's eye—that handsome, kindly face, those benevolent eyes, that spirited shock of white hair standing up on end, and all at once he understood that Ercole was the only man in the world to whom he might have confided his secret. He was convinced now that the Captain could have helped him. His death struck him as an evil omen.

As the hour of midnight approached he was breathless with fear. "Why am I so terrified?" he groaned. "Why am I so terrified? Never have I been so terrified as I am today!"

And once more he tried to pray. "Oh Lord God, let it be the last time . . . I implore Thee! I have done nothing wrong. I am innocent . . . Bandini himself says that he thinks me a good fellow. . . . Everybody is kind to me. . . . Why art Thou so hard on me? Why me? I implore Thee, let it be for the last time, the very last time ... dear Lord, I ...

The chimes rang out the hour and he could not finish.

Peppina came through the garden leading the dog. "Just look, madam," she called from the terrace, "he was lying outside the front door, and slipped in when Hassan opened it. He ran past little Hassan. He's frightened," she added with a laugh.

Claudia appeared at the garden door. The dog ran toward her, and jumped gently up to her, then stood still, wagging his tail, his eyes fixed on her. She stroked him.

"What do you want here, Cambyses?" she said in caressing tones. "Are you looking for your master? Is that it? ... He isn't here." And she went into her room, the dog following. She rang the bell and the mulatto glided in.

"Here is the Archduke's dog who has come to see us, Caligula," she said. "He's looking for his master. Just catch him and take him back to the Palace."

The mulatto came forward, but the dog sprang toward the alcove and snapped at Caligula's outstretched hand with a low growl. "Come along! Come with me!" coaxed the mulatto in his shrill, oily voice.

But the dog only growled and crept under the bed.

The mulatto squinted at Claudia, shook his head gravely from side to side, and raised his hand. "The dog," he muttered mysteriously, "the dog!"

"Are you frightened of him?" laughed Claudia.

The mulatto continued to shake his head, and spreading out his fingers, waved his hand in the air, looking anxiously at his mistress.

Claudia took no notice of his gesticulations. "Well then, let him stop where he is," she concluded, "his master will find him here when he comes."

The mulatto left the room and the dog immediately crept out from his hiding place.

"You're a cunning creature!" cried Claudia, laughing in surprise. "Anyone can see what you want." The dog gazed up at her and wagged his tail.

"Yes, I understand you. You almost speak, don't you?

You want to stay with me," she said. Bending over, she stroked him. "How could I fail to understand that? All right, Cambyses, you may stay with me." He lay quietly down at her feet.

Presently, when Claudia was being dressed and the finishing touches put to her toilet by Peppina and Carletta, Cambyses sat by her, following every one of her movements with his eyes, and jealously observing everything the two servants did, as though he felt it incumbent upon him to protect Claudia from any ill-treatment.

Still keeping close beside her, he entered the room in which the Archduke was waiting.

"What do you think of your dog?" Claudia asked him with a smile. "Aren't you surprised, my lord?"

"So that is where the brute was!" exclaimed the Archduke frowning.

Claudia was highly amused by the Prince's vexation. "Yes, Cambyses was with me and he's not a brute, but a good clever dog."

"He has again been away from home for two days,"

said the Archduke, glancing disapprovingly down at the dog.

"For two days?" laughed Claudia. "Well, he has only come to me today. But he must have been here all the time. He came and paid me a visit early this morning, and has not stirred from my side since. I have grown quite used to him."

"If you like him, keep him," said the Archduke with a majestic wave of his hand. "I give him to you."

"Really?"

The Archduke nodded.

Claudia kissed the palm of her hand and blew on it, as though she wanted to waft the kiss into the Archduke's face. "How lovely!" she cried in delight, passing a hand over the dog's head.

"You won't get much pleasure out of the cur," said the Archduke with a smile. "He's a poor sort of present. He disappears every other minute, no one knows where."

Claudia dropped on her knees and put her arm round the dog's neck. "Are you going to run away from me too, Cambyses?" she asked with her face quite close to his. "You won't, will you? I should be dreadfully upset if you did." The dog nestled up to her and pressed his head against her breast.

Presently as Claudia was sitting at dinner with the Archduke, the dog lay at her feet, and overheard everything.

"So it's tomorrow?" Claudia enquired.

"Unfortunately, yes . . ." the Archduke replied.

"What time?"

"A little before midday. But we shall not go very far tomorrow. We are giving a farewell breakfast . . . the Grand Duke is accompanying me as far as Prato."

"How soon will you forget me?"

"Not for a very long time."

"But you will forget me in the end," said Claudia softly.

"As long as I retain my youth," the Archduke replied simply, "I shall not forget you, because I never had enough of you, and I shall often long for you."

Her laugh was like a short song. "And what about when you are old?"

"When I am old," he replied with the same simplicity, "I shall probably not forget you either, for then it will be a delight to think of you, and remember that once upon a time it happened."

Claudia laughed louder. "Ah, woe is me!" she cried cheerfully, "how pat you have it all! How nice and tidy your heart is!"

And they went on talking, the dog lying at their feet, his head raised, listening.

Later on when they left the table and withdrew to the bedroom, the dog slipped in with them. They noticed that he had done so only when he suddenly pushed himself between them.

"Oh Cambyses!" cried the Archduke. "He must clear out. He can't stop here, can he?" And retreating a step, he looked enquiringly at Claudia.

"Certainly not." She shook her head. "His eyes are like a man's. One is not alone when he is there."

The Archduke went to the door and opened it a little. "Here, Cambyses!" He exclaimed, "Out with you!

The dog did not stir.

With a laugh Claudia went to the garden door and opened it. "Come along, Cambyses, there's a good dog!"

Still the dog did not stir.

"A stick!" exclaimed the Archduke, looking round. "Or a whip!"

The dog gave a short bark. It sounded like a contradiction.

"No, don't beat him!" Claudia was touched by his bark. "He'll go all right. Perhaps Caligula will be able to take him out."

The Archduke thrust out his underlip. "I refuse to be provoked just now," he said, and stretching out his arms he went toward Claudia.

The dog flew at him, baring his fangs.

The Archduke started back. "What's the matter now?" he exclaimed, trying to hide his fright under a laugh and making an attempt to get past the dog. But once more the animal barred his way and his snarl became a deep growl.

The Archduke tried to kick out at him. "Just you wait . . . !" he cried. But the dog became frantic with rage and snapped at him and the Archduke felt the brute's sharp teeth through his stocking. Beside himself with rage, he bent forward meaning to give the dog a blow with his fist, but Cambyses reared up on his hind legs and with his forepaws pressing on the Archduke's shoulders, forced him to straighten himself and then kept fast hold of him, snarling, snapping, and opening his huge jaws in mad fury.

Claudia screamed.

The Archduke reeled backward with the dog's forepaws still on him, twisting his blanched, livid face this way and that, in an effort to escape from the foaming mouth and gleaming teeth of the dog whose breath steamed into his nostrils. Suddenly he was seized with panic. He groped clumsily round the dog's neck, trying to seize it, but quick as lightning the animal snapped at him and bit him. Blood poured from the burning wound. Like one possessed the dog hung round his neck, barking, yapping, howling in his face, pressing him toward the door with such terrific force that he was obliged to yield step by step.

In a paroxysm of fear the Archduke suddenly began to grasp that it was a matter of life and death, and he groped madly about his girdle. At last he gripped the dagger he was looking for. Drawing it stealthily from its sheath, he summoned up all his strength and plunged the blade deep into the dog's body at the point where the neck leaves the breast and the shoulder.

Only a stifled cry was heard as the dog collapsed, dropping so heavily at the Archduke's feet that he wrenched the handle of the dagger from his grasp as he fell and lay quivering on the floor.

Again Claudia uttered a piercing shriek.

And they stood facing each other, pale as death, panting and beside themselves with fear.

The Archduke looked down at the dog who lay stretched out on the floor, quivering slightly. "Brute!" He was foaming with rage. "Ravening brute!" And he shuddered with horror.

"Oh, put him out of sight! Put him out of sight!" cried Claudia, quite beside herself, holding her hands to her eyes and sobbing aloud.

"Well call someone, for heaven's sake . . . the bell is there . . ." said the Archduke, speaking again with some effort.

"No, no! I don't want to call anyone. No!" Her voice became a wail. "I don't want anyone to come! For Heaven's sake put him out of sight at once!" She seemed to have taken leave of her senses.

The Archduke pushed the dog along in front of him with his foot. The blood was pouring in a thick stream from his neck, leaving a broad red streak across the carpet. The door leading to the garden stood open and the Archduke pushed the limp heavy body out on to the terrace. "Scoundrel!" he muttered, angrily closing the door.

"The curtain!" begged Claudia. "Now the curtain! There's the cord.... Yes... that one!" The Archduke tugged mechanically at the tassel, the gay figured tapestry slid forward and closed and all that met the eye was a woven wall-hanging of many colors, depicting an Arcadian scene in which blissful deities were condescending to consort with the beautiful lovelorn daughters of men.

· · ·

When Caligula, the mulatto, stole across the terrace at dawn, to spy around, he found the young stranger stretched out close to Claudia's door.

He gazed down on the wretched man who had twice pushed his way violently into the house and nodded with a broad silent grin on his face. Suddenly his dull eyes gleamed with joy as he saw the dagger with its glittering bejewelled handle sticking out between the young man's neck and shoulder. The first tender rays of the rising sun sparkled in the diamonds, rubies and pearls with which the handle was studded, making it look more like a precious bauble than a deadly weapon.

Caligula bent down. He wanted to extricate the weapon from the wound and secure the tempting treasure for himself. But with a low cry he suddenly shrank back.

Lucas was still breathing!

Terrified out of his wits the mulatto stood for a moment rooted to the spot and gazed round. Then forming a sudden resolve, he darted toward the door and began to drum on the window-panes with his soft fingers. He also kicked the wooden panels with his slippered feet and called Claudia's name in a shrill terrified falsetto.

After a while the curtain inside the room was drawn aside.

Caligula pressed his fat mulatto face against the window-pane, and tried to see inside the room.

The Archduke had gone and Claudia was alone.

With strange convulsive warning gestures and signs, Caligula began to perform a dance which was blood-curdling in its silence.

When Claudia appeared on the threshold he could only point down at the wounded man. "There! . . . there! . . . there!" was all he could stammer out.

Claudia gazed down horror-stricken. At once she saw the connection between the dog and the man. She did not understand the secret of their identity, nor did she waste time trying to think it out. Nevertheless, long after the event she at last understood the dog's mad fury and knew what the young man imprisoned in the form of the dog must have gone through that night.

"Carry him to my bed!" she commanded. "Take great care . . . do you hear, Caligula . . . take great care!"

The mulatto lifted the unconscious youth in his arms, as easily as though he were a child, and, after carefully undressing him, put him to bed. Claudia was convulsed by passionate sobs. At last, pulling herself together, she went up to Caligula.

"Listen," she whispered, "listen! You must save him. Do you understand? You must!"

She caught hold of his wrists, and he could feel her whole body quivering as she implored him.

"If I can," he muttered, releasing himself from her grasp.

But she caught hold of him again. "You can . . . I know you can heal wounds. . . . You must save him! I know you are a past master at healing. . . . You can ask anything you like of me!" And she sank almost unconscious on his breast.

Releasing himself from her once more, he went over to the wounded man. A moment later he left the room, but returned soon afterward with all manner of vials, bottles and instruments. His broad back concealed from Claudia what he was doing to Lucas Grassi.

After a while he took the dagger to Claudia, who was sitting huddled up on the floor by the window. She sprang to her feet, wrapped the weapon in a white silk cloth, locked it in a cabinet and turning quickly to Caligula, whispered, "Silence! No one must suspect anything of this!"

The mulatto folded his arms. "No one . . ." he repeated in a whisper.

Claudia staggered quickly toward him. "Tell me . . . will he die?" she whispered when she was close beside him.

"Perhaps!" replied Caligula softly.

She either did not or would not hear, but pressed him further. "Tell me . . . will he live?"

"Perhaps!" replied Caligula as before.

Toward midday the wounded man grew restless. He had not yet recovered consciousness, but was throwing his arms and legs about.

At that very hour the Archduke left the city of Florence.

Whereupon Lucas Grassi lay still and quiet, breathing heavily with his eyes closed.

Claudia sat on the bed watching him. "Oh my beloved . . . !" she sighed from time to time.

Now and again Caligula would come in and give the invalid all manner of strange treatments.

When it had been dark for some time, Lucas woke up. Glancing about him in confusion, he recognized Claudia in the flickering light of the candle. He closed his eyes and was lost in thought. Had he been dreaming? Had he really experienced that terrible scene?

His hand groped for the wound which gave a twinge as he touched it. His fingers felt the bandage.

"Claudia!" he said very softly.

"Beloved!" Eagerly she bent over him and tried to kiss him.

"No, not yet!" he implored. And as she drew back, he added, "Is it nearly midnight?"

"Why?"

"Is it nearly midnight?" she could hear the terror in his sick, feeble voice.

"Yes, beloved," she replied in tender comforting tones. "Yes... nearly." Whereupon, overcome with emotion, repentance and longing for forgiveness, she added, "What you have suffered ... for my sake ... but explain to me, I do not understand at all ... you must have faith in me ... and tell me."

"Wait!" he implored, and she could tell from his voice that his terror had increased.

She said no more and Lucas too lay silent, but his breath seemed to come faster and faster.

The hour crawled by painfully on leaden feet.

At last the soft metallic chimes of the cathedral campanile echoed through the room.... Midnight!

At the first stroke Lucas started. The other church bells chimed in and he counted twelve strokes.

Nothing stirred within him. No metamorphosis tore him away.

A great outburst of joy flooded his being. "I am

free! I am free!" he cried, laughing and sobbing at once. And when he could say no more his smiling lips continued to whisper. . . . "Free . . . free . . . free!"

"May I kiss you now?" asked Claudia.

He gazed into her face, which was close above his own. "Kiss me!" he begged. And as her lips met his, he seemed to gain fresh strength. "Ah . . ." he murmured, "how it all happened . . . I do not even know myself . . . nor can I explain it. . . . I was very poor . . . very poor. . . . I longed terribly for things, and was very unhappy . . . very. . . . Yes, I was a dog in my misery, and in my poverty . . . a dog. . . ." He stopped, overcome by weakness. "A dog . . ." he whispered presently, "Perhaps every poor man . . . a dog. . . ." Once more he opened his eyes and gazed at his beloved. "But now . . . I am free . . . free . . . free and happy."

And he sank into a deep sleep.

Claudia turned to the mulatto, who had hastened to the room and stood gazing on the sleeping man shaking his head.

"Will he die?" she enquired anxiously.

Caligula gave a faint shrug of his shoulders. "Perhaps..." he said almost inaudibly.

"Will he live?" implored Claudia, gliding swiftly up to him.

The mulatto gazed over his shoulder into the distance and whispered, "Perhaps."